KING OF THE MOUNTAINS

SEASONS OF FAE BOOK 1

ELIZABETH FROST

For all those people who believed in me.
And for everyone who's fallen in love with the fae

1

———

"You said she would be easy to convince!" A hissed voice drifted through her window from the garden.

A second replied, "No, I said she would be easy to find."

Damned fools. Morgan put down her spoon and glared out the window to her left. The fire cracked and hurled a small ember in the direction of the speakers.

She didn't have guests. No one wandered into the haunted wood where the witch—as the townsfolk so lovingly called her—lived. She might turn them into a toad, or worse, make warts grow on their genitals.

Her cauldron hung suspended over the fire. Its contents were black and oozing, popping now and then like a tar bed. She'd rather continue to watch her newest creation, so it didn't turn into a creature of its own making.

But now, she had to deal with these unknown callers.

Visitors.

She stalked through the single room cabin. Vines hung through the slats in the ceiling. They tangled in her hair and shoulders, trying to stop her from going to the door. They whispered in her ears, "No, Morgan. Just pretend you aren't here!"

The vines were always terrified of unfamiliar people. Probably because the last time she'd brought a stranger here was the man who worked on her roof. He'd ripped the poor dears up by their roots and tossed them into the trash.

Of course, he'd been human and couldn't hear them screaming.

She passed her hammock in the corner with rainbow-colored quilts draped over the edge. A small table, beneath the only window in the entire earthbound cottage, provided a view into her garden. And a way for her to see the three people standing atop the spinach.

They had no idea what wrath they'd brought upon themselves. That spinach was stubborn! She'd spent the better part of a month trying to convince it to grow.

If they wanted to see her, so be it. But leave her damn garden alone.

She threw open the door and braced herself on the frame. Her glare should have seared flesh from bone. Her snarl would have scared any human wandering where they shouldn't.

The people in her garden weren't human, though. The man in front raised his hand as though he were reaching to knock on the door. His yellowed mustache drooped rather impressively toward the ground. The tips swung with his surprise the moment she appeared.

The woman behind him had eyes bigger than teacups. She blinked the wrong way, horizontal instead of vertical. Considering her ears were pointed, Morgan could already guess she was a faerie. What kind, Morgan didn't know. Witches stayed away from the fae.

Far in the back, the last man shifted under the weight of her gaze. He was far too hairy. Fur poked up from his collar, smattered the backs of his hands, and even poked out underneath the fine suit he wore.

Morgan pointed to the last. "You steal a single vegetable from my garden, werewolf, and I'll wear your hide."

He held up his hands. "I wouldn't dare."

She couldn't hazard a guess why these creatures were here. She lived far away from the rest of the world. No one wandered into the forests of upper State New York, especially these woods.

The locals spread myths about her cabin. They whispered tales of the witch who would gift love charms but steal hearts. And not in the good way. For modern day folks, they were a superstitious bunch. Far be it from Morgan to correct their claims when they were true. Their lovers came to her for charms. She gave them whatever they desired.

It wasn't her fault humans didn't understand magic came with a price.

The strangers stared at her, their eyes wide and their jaws agape.

Morgan wasn't a "beauty", nor did she wish to be. Her long black hair was tangled in near dreadlocks from disregard, not intention. What little eyeliner she wore had dripped down her face from sweat and work. She couldn't remember the last time she'd bathed either, but she was busy! Who had time to bathe?

The man with the mustache cleared his throat. "Madame Morgan Lefair, we have come seeking your help and guidance."

She narrowed her gaze. What was he? The other two were faerie and werewolf, but this one eluded her.

She leaned close, still holding onto the door frame, and inhaled. The brassy punch of copper filled her nostrils, metallic and bitter. "Ah," she murmured. "Hello, vampire."

If it were possible for the man to pale even further, he did. "Yes, Madame. I am a vampire, my name is Louis. The fae is Aster, and the werewolf is Russell."

As if she cared what their names were. She wanted them off her property. Their names didn't matter as long as they were fast runners. Morgan continued to stare at them in silence until the three rocked back and forth on their heels like nervous children.

Louis cleared his throat again. "Madame, we come seeking your help."

"I heard you the first time."

"Perhaps we might come in?" His gaze flicked over her shoulder and into the shadows of her home. "I'm afraid this isn't a conversation we should have outside."

"Why not?" Her gruff tone should have given him a hint. She wanted them all to leave. However, their situation must be dire. None of them were budging, no matter how rude she was.

"It's a matter of great importance, and we cannot be certain our conversation will remain private out in the open."

Morgan quirked a brow. "I think you've got the wrong house then, vamp. I don't do important or private."

"You're the only one who can help us." His voice took on a pleading edge.

She hated it when they begged. Grumbling, she moved aside and pointed into the cabin. "Come on then. Make it quick, I don't have all day."

The three rushed inside like she would slam the door shut on their fingers if they took too long. She didn't crush their hands, but Morgan let it slam shut behind them just to see them jump.

"Oh," the faerie woman gasped. "It's lovely in here."

"Did you think the witch would live in a dirt hovel?" Morgan asked, then made her way back to the cauldron. "That only happened in the old days, and only because witches were poor."

Her ancestors would have preferred wooden floors as well. They would have loved talking with the plants and using magic in every corner of their house. None of them wanted to live in shacks at the edge of bogs, desperately trying to make ends meet.

Aster reached up and touched a finger to one vine. The traitorous plant coiled around the tip, stroking against her for a moment before releasing.

Plants. They always had a thing for the fae.

Aster turned with a bright grin on her face. "You're a green witch!"

Morgan bared her teeth in a snarl. "Hedge witch."

"Forgive me." Aster paled, her voice light but clearly terrified. "I didn't mean to insult you."

Why were faeries always so delicate? She could hurt their feelings in an instant, and they melted into the floor.

Morgan sighed, picked up her spoon, and turned back to the cauldron. The blast of warm air from her fire made her feel more comfortable, or perhaps it was that she had turned away from the strangers invading her space. "It's fine, faerie. Why don't you all sit down?"

She could almost feel their confusion. Where did she want them to sit? There was no sofa or chairs, nor was there a living room in her home.

This was her favorite part. A wicked side of her soul grinned as she whispered a small incantation. "Vines grow and leaves bend, make a seat for my new friends."

All the plants in her ceiling reached down with long tendrils of vines and roots. She could hear the creaking and slithering as they coiled together to make a couch. Sometimes it was comfortable, sometimes it wasn't. Morgan rarely sat on whatever they made, anyway. She had her hammock or soft moss outside.

Another grinding sound suggested all three had sat down at once. They were rather obedient strangers at least.

Giving the cauldron one last swirl, she set the spoon down

on its rest and turned around. She crossed her arms over her chest. "What is it then? Do you need some kind of potion to make a child born of three, not two? I've done it before, but I can't promise the babe will be normal."

Again, the faerie's face turned white as snow. "No! No, please don't do that."

Hm, interesting. Morgan pointed between the three of them. "Clearly there's something happening here. Why else would you come into my wood?"

The vampire was the one to speak again. Louis crossed his legs, placed his hands atop them and said, "We need you to save the world."

A lengthy pause extended between them. Morgan waited for him to continue, to say anything other than that ridiculous claim. When he didn't say a single thing for long heartbeats, she burst into laughter.

Deep chortles made her stomach ache and tears run down her cheeks. "Save the world?" she repeated, then erupted into hysterical laughter once more. Calming herself, she wiped a finger under her eyes and let out one last snort. "Really, that's a good one. Tell me another, vamp."

No one else laughed. Instead, the strangers were watching her. Expecting... something.

Morgan sighed, "All right. You think I can save the world. Let's make a list of the reasons no one possibly could." She ticked off her fingers as she went. "We've destroyed natural resources in favor of building concrete jungles. Our political leaders are all corrupt. People only care for themselves. Not to mention humans run the planet, not those of us with magic."

"We're not asking you to help with any of those," Louis replied.

She waited again, but they still didn't continue. Exasperated, she tossed her hands in the air. "Well then spit it out! In my opinion, the world doesn't need saving. It needs a reset."

The werewolf—what was his name? Rudolph?—spoke next. "That's what we believe will happen. If we don't stop the faerie kings from ascending to their thrones, they will wipe the earth clean of everyone but the magical community."

"So?" She blurted the word out before she could stop herself. "Sounds like an excellent plan."

Louis's foot dropped off his knee with a loud thump. "We need humans."

"No." She pointed at him. "You need humans. I don't need them at all."

"They run this planet. They're an important part of how the world runs, we cannot let them all die off. It would be detrimental to the realm!"

"I don't eat humans."

His eyes bulged in surprise. "Neither do I."

Morgan tilted her head to the side and gave him a censoring look. "Oh I know the legends about your kind, vampire. We all know you eat animals now, but if given the chance, you'd all switch back to that warm human blood in a second. And I for one question whether you're all actually surviving on a rather bland diet."

If he hadn't wanted something from her, Morgan felt certain the vampire would have launched himself across the room. He clenched his hands into fists and his eyes glazed into a red glow. The beast he kept tamed wanted its time with her.

She hadn't fought a vampire in a very long time. Let him try his best to kill her. She'd show him what a witch could do.

The werewolf was the one who interrupted their staring contest. "Stop this, please. If you would just listen to us, then perhaps we could convince you otherwise."

"Shut up, Randall," she grumbled.

"Actually, it's Russell," he corrected. "Madame Lefair, the faerie kings won't just kill off the humans. They will remake the world in their own image, run by the fae and enslaving the rest of us. I don't suppose you've heard the prophecy before?"

Oh god, prophecies. She steepled her fingers and pressed them against her forehead. "Please tell me you don't believe in some ridiculous story one of my ancestors made up."

"It's not just a story," Aster replied. The faerie woman leaned forward until her bottom was barely on the seat. "Morgana le Fay and Nimue were the first to declare what would happen if the faerie kings took their true and rightful thrones."

"My namesake never liked Nimue. They wouldn't have worked together like that." Such a prophecy would require scrying, and Morgan had talked to her greatest of grandmother's before. Morgana would sooner have cut off Nimue's head than stare into a looking glass with her.

"But they did," Aster replied. "It's less of a prophecy and more of a warning. The faerie kings are far too dangerous to let wander and expose their magic. Nimue was the first to ensure it didn't happen. That's why she gave Arthur the sword."

A vine slid down from the ceiling and touched the top of Morgan's head. Her anger was disturbing the plants. She reached up, touched the tendril, and gave it a single pet. "You're speaking of my heritage, fae. Don't try to educate me on the history of witches."

Rufus stood and took a couple steps toward her, only stopping when her hand twitched. "I don't know how to explain to you what we fear will happen. But these faerie kings, they have to be controlled."

"And what do you think I can do?" Morgan turned back to her cauldron. "Get out of my house. I'm not interested in your theories."

Silence rang behind her like the ticking of a bomb. Louis was the one who finally broke the silence. "I don't want to force you, Morgan. But we know what you did to those boys who wandered into your garden five years ago. We know where they're buried, and we'll call the police."

She stiffened. They knew? She had buried her tracks so deep with magic, not even a witch would know what she had done.

Swallowing, she forced her shoulders to relax and reached for her spoon again. Morgan stirred the cauldron and asked, "Whatever do you mean?"

"They meant harm, didn't they? You wouldn't kill teenagers unless you had to, we understand that. I could smell them underneath the hedges, Morgan. All I have to do is call the police, and they'll put you behind bars for the rest of your life."

"No human prison could hold me." Her hand shook with the next swirling stir.

Aster hummed in the back of her throat. "No, it couldn't. Most magical prisons could, however, and we're more than happy to call them as well."

She stared down at the black liquid in her cauldron and realized there was no way for her to get out of this. They had her by the throat.

A magical prison was a death sentence.

Her hands shook so badly she dropped her spoon into the black mire. It devoured the utensil, a spell gone wrong.

They had her, and they knew it. She had to help them, or they would destroy her life.

She heaved a deep sigh, turned around, and crossed her arms over her chest. "Fine. What do you want me to do?"

The three of them shared a single look before they replied in unison, "You need to kill a faerie king."

2

The two men disappeared as soon as she agreed to work for them. They raced away from her property like the hounds of hell were on their tails. They might be. She still hadn't decided if she wanted to send a few beasts after the strangers who had come in and turned her life upside down.

She glared at the faerie who remained. Aster was by far the weakest of the three. Why would they leave the fragile, insignificant creature to Morgan's whims?

The faerie blushed bright pink and eyed the door. "I'm supposed to help you prepare for the king."

"Why am I preparing for someone you want me to kill?" Morgan didn't need to look nice for the man. She needed him to lie down and accept her blade across his throat.

She hadn't killed anyone in a very long time. Five years, to be precise. And even then, it was only to keep herself safe.

She'd always remember them, drunk and stumbling through her woods. The way the first boy had fumbled with his belt buckle because his fingers were too slow to do what his brain wanted. Five inexperienced young men against a single woman. They'd thought she would be easy prey to leave behind in the woods where no one would find her.

Now, they fed her hedges. The plants had grown twice their height in just the few years of food from their bodies.

Aster toyed with her fingers. "You're supposed to go now," she whispered.

"Why?"

"Because the faerie kings are very volatile and we don't know when he might take the throne." She picked at the raw skin around her fingernails. "He's not predictable."

"No faerie is." Morgan could argue the value of patience until she was blue in the face, but these people wanted her job done sooner rather than later.

Sighing, she strode toward the back of the room. "Fine, if you want me to be appealing to the faerie king, I will be. What does he like?"

The innocent creature behind her squeaked, "Um, whatever do you mean, Madame?"

"I mean he must have a type and I can be the temptress who kills him in his bed."

Morgan reached her hands up and cleared her mind. She envisioned her closet, full of clothing from now and ancient times. Back in the days when witches had been hunted all the way to modern day where women could wear pants.

The closet shimmered into view, replacing her hammock bed covered in pillows and blankets. Instead, the entire wall of the cottage was filled with clothing.

Aster whispered, "Wow."

"Magic," Morgan replied. "It has its uses."

"I thought witches didn't use magic often?" Aster asked. "I've only met one in my life and she said magic had its price."

Morgan shrugged. "It does. But my other spell was already ruined, so I might as well sacrifice that to see what I have in my closet. Now, what does the faerie king desire in a woman?"

The faerie took her sweet time in responding before she answered, "Pretty?"

Of course, that was the only thing she could think of. All faeries liked pretty things. They were practically dragons in their desire for glimmering lights, sparkling fabrics, and anything glowing.

Morgan could cover herself in gems that glittered in the sunlight, and she would catch a thousand faeries. All she needed was to look like something expensive.

Snorting, she shifted through a few of the outfits. Some of them were older, a peasant dress from the 1800s, a Victorian gown from when she'd been more important to the humans. Morgan had learned her lesson rather quick when they'd tried to burn her. Stay away from humans at all costs.

No, none of those would work. The faerie king wouldn't want someone to step out of history and entice him. He'd been there, lived that.

"What is the faerie king like then?" she asked. "Tell me about him. Maybe I can get an idea of his type."

Aster skipped to her side, all of a sudden infinitely bubbly and happy. "Oh! I love telling stories!"

And Morgan loved her peace. The last thing she wanted was a happy faerie starting to sweat glitter on all her things. It was impossible to get that shit off the floor. It stuck like glue.

They know about the boys, she thought. They will dig up your garden and throw you into a prison for the rest of your life where you will live in hell. Do not test the faerie.

Instead of arguing or making fun of the burst of happiness, Morgan waited for the faerie to speak.

Aster plopped herself down on the floor at Morgan's side. She wrapped her arms around her knees and eyed the clothing as though they held the answer to the world. "You're going after the Mountain King. He's very prickly, like thorns on a rose bush. Nasty."

"Thorns on a rose bush aren't bad. They protect the rose from bugs."

Aster clicked her tongue. "Then not a rose bush. Maybe more like a thistle plant, with the burrs that stick to you and hurt something fierce?"

Morgan liked the man already. He frightened his people into following his every whim. She could respect that. "Okay, so he's more dangerous than the other faeries. Not into sparkly things?" she asked while holding her breath. *Please don't want me to dress up in glitter and pasties.*

"No," Aster replied vehemently. "He likes nothing that's faerie, really. The Mountain King lives far away in the wilderness where he's surrounded himself with only the most loyal of his people. He's very disconcerting."

"And women?" She'd never met a faerie who didn't surround himself with a harem to do with as he pleased. They were sexual creatures at their core.

"Not that I've ever seen," Aster replied. "He values power more than beauty. But mostly, he just wants to be left alone."

Why did they have to send her to kill someone she might like? Morgan felt the same pain as this mysterious king.

Such a shame he had to die.

She reached deep into the recesses of her wardrobe and pulled out an outfit she thought might work. The white button-down shirt was rather demure, although she would leave it open far past the swells of her breasts. Black leather pants would hug her curves in a distracting way, while the black knee-high boots were modern.

If the faerie king wanted to be left alone, then she would be more than happy to bring the modern world to him. Let him see just how much the world had changed.

"What do you think?" She held the outfit up to Aster.

The faerie woman shrugged. "Hard to tell. I'd suggest sneaking up on him and slitting his throat in the shadows, but the other two didn't think that would work. He's protected from every angle."

And Morgan was no assassin.

Sneaking up on anyone just to slice their throat wasn't her specialty. She could curse them from here to their dead grandparent. That's where her talents lay.

So the other two were right. Make friends with the man first and then kill him. That was the best way to get close to the faerie king. Even if she hated to admit Rudolph was right about anything.

Werewolves. She'd never liked them.

Morgan held the outfit against her body and closed her eyes. The spell was easy to create. She sacrificed a few strands of hair and half her left pinky nail.

Cool air flowed down her torso as though she had stepped under a waterfall. It brushed through the snarls of her hair, smoothing them out into ebony curls, soft and bouncy. Magic scrubbed the dirt away and left her face fresh and clean. It melted the clothing onto her form and dressed her like the most loyal of servants.

Aster let out another, "Oh!"

When the magic had finished, Morgan opened her eyes. "Never seen witch magic up close, have you?"

"Not like that," the faerie replied. "That was beautiful!"

She wished she still had such love for magic. Morgan vaguely remembered a time in her life when she had been enthralled by her teachers. They had levitated items into the air, and she had lost all breath in her lungs.

Now, magic was just part of her life. She didn't even think about the hovering cauldron, the magical closet, or how she could wish herself clean. Such things were basic magic.

She was just a hedge witch. Other witches were capable of much more powerful spells than she. They could move mountains if they wished.

Morgan kept herself and her home clean.

Clearing her throat and mind of such thoughts, she gestured to the door. "I have things to do. If you want me to kill the faerie king, I only have a week. The witch council is holding a gathering I cannot miss."

"But, Madame Lefair, I can only assume killing a faerie king would take longer than that?" Aster asked.

"I guess we'll see," Morgan replied. She didn't intend to take that long.

Walk into the palace like something out of a storybook. Charm the king into giving her a few minutes alone under the pretense she'd always wanted to see what faerie men hid underneath their trousers. And then voila. Kill the man.

Her hands weren't shaking because she feared taking another life. They were shaking because she hadn't been clean in a long time and she didn't feel like herself. That was all.

Aster trailed behind her as they both left the house. Morgan waited, but Aster just stood in the middle of her garden, staring at her with those wide, strangely blinking eyes.

"Well?" Morgan said.

Aster blinked again.

Oh Heavens and Hell, she hated faeries. "Where are we going, fae?"

Aster jumped, lifting her hands and pressing them against her cheeks. "Oh my goodness! I'm so sorry, Madame Lefair. Into the woods, wherever you'd be comfortable with me opening a portal."

She had to hold in the groan of disgust. A portal? A faerie portal? On her property?

Faerie portals were notoriously difficult to close because they connected with nature to open up. The trees would be reluctant to let go of the magic feeding into their roots. She'd have to deal with countless wandering fae until she could find the right spell to close the damn portal.

"Is there no other way?" she asked.

"Not to get to the Mountain King's home. He lives in a land between lands, one he made for himself and the closest of his people." Aster replied.

"Really?" Impressive. She'd never heard of such magic.

"Really." The faerie woman rolled up a single sleeve. Her skin, pale as parchment paper, had bright green veins at the wrist. "At your order, Madame."

"What are you doing to open the portal?"

"My blood will do it. Faerie blood spilled on green grass will summon the Mountain King's help." Aster met her gaze and shrugged. "I'm of his court. That's why they left me with you. I can get you to him."

Well, it made some kind of morbid sense. Morgan would want to keep the portal closer to her so she could put some kind of spell around it and contain the beasties who wreaked havoc wherever they went. She pointed to the back end of the garden, still within the wooden fence surrounding her property. "There, then."

Aster skipped to the place she pointed. Without a single moment of hesitation, the faerie slit a long cut in her palm and held it over the ground. "Mountain King, I call upon thee. Save one of your own and allow me safe passage to your haven in the wilds."

As Morgan watched, three heavy drops of verdant blood dripped from Aster's hand and onto the ground. The grass undulated, and the ground rolled. Then, a shimmering wall rose from the ground to about ten feet high.

She licked her lips and nodded. "Impressive."

"Thank you," Aster replied with a happy giggle. "Now, all you have to do is go through the portal, find the king, and kill him."

Right, like that would be so easy when he had surrounded

himself with faeries. They made it seem like a hedge witch could do this in her sleep.

Morgan stepped close to the portal and furrowed her brow. "You never explained why you came to me and not a more powerful witch."

"Oh I don't know. You'd have to ask Louis that question, he's the one who found you." The faerie leaned down and picked a handful of grass. She pressed it against the wound and the blades laced through her flesh like gauze.

"So helpful," Morgan murmured.

It made little sense. If there were more powerful witches, and there were hundreds, why would they come to her? Because she was the only one they could blackmail? She also doubted that.

She turned back to Aster and closed her hands into fists. "You know, I could just kill you now and run. Your friends wouldn't be able to find me."

"You could try," Aster replied. "Faeries are harder to kill than you might think."

"I've killed a few in my day."

"I remember the stories. You're a lot older than you look, Morgan Lefair." She grinned, all sharp teeth and faerie magic. "But so am I."

Aster reached out, her hand quicker than lightning. She thumped her palm against the center of Morgan's chest and shoved her hard. The force thrust her through the portal and into the realm of the Mountain King.

3

Morgan fell through the portal and landed on her butt. The impact zinged through her hipbones and down into her knees.

Hissing, she reached back and massaged the base of her spine. "I'm getting too old for this kind of treatment." Although, she supposed her age wasn't an excuse anymore.

When one was over five hundred years old, age wasn't worth tracking.

She rolled onto her feet and stretched her arms up over her head. Portal travel always made her feel strange. The electricity of magic ricocheted through her entire being, making her hair stand on end for hours. Not to mention it always made her stomach queasy.

"You couldn't have told me where to find the Mountain King?" she shot back at the portal. "You had to shove me through before getting all the information?"

Find the Mountain King, they said. Kill him with nothing more than her own magic. Surely that should be easy enough?

If she got her hands around that stupid werewolf or Louis's neck, she would squeeze so hard they realized she was a better killer than they thought. Of course, they wouldn't let her. The chances of seeing those fools again were slim to none.

She didn't have weapons in her home. Guns went haywire around magic. Swords were far too medieval and had never worked against faeries to begin with. So she'd have to rely on her own magic.

In that, her strange new friends were correct. They had sent her into the portal with the strongest weapon she had.

Herself.

Morgan turned around and eyed the overgrown forest beyond. "Find the king," she repeated. "Where oh where am I going to find a king?"

In a castle if she knew faeries. And she did, because she'd studied them very early in her witchcraft. They had fascinated Morgan. The natural allure of the fae was tantalizing to a young witch.

But faeries only liked beautiful things. They devoured beauty as she did ice cream. Anything less than perfect was beneath them.

He was definitely in a castle.

Her sturdy knee-high boots would come in handy in the middle of a forest. The trees here were larger than ones she'd ever seen, even back when she'd first been born. Morgan reached out a hand and touched the bark of the nearest one.

Flashes of memories burst behind her closed eyes. People who had walked past the ancient being. Creatures who made their homes within its branches and deep inside its trunk. This tree was more than just old. It had survived the dawning of time.

"Hello," she whispered. "Do you mind if I wander a bit?"

The trunk groaned, and the tree leaned in. Just enough for her to know the tree had agreed, although she got a flash of warning behind her eyes as well. Red blood splattered on the trunk of a tree. The dead body dragged deep into the earth by roots impaled through the creature's chest.

The forest refused to stand by while an attacker came into its realm. Such a shame. She'd have to run past them back to the portal when she finished killing the king.

Morgan removed her hand and gave the tree a nod. "I hear you, ancient friend. I understand."

Unfortunately, she just wouldn't be able to abide by the forest's rule. No matter how much it wanted to protect its king, she had to protect herself first.

The first rule of witchcraft. Always take care of yourself, then others.

Morgan left the portal and started off through the woods. She tried to walk as straight as possible, but she didn't worry too much about finding the portal again. A beacon in her little cottage always called to her. If she wanted to return home at any point, it would guide her back to the portal.

Birds burst into flight overhead, their bodies covered in crystal gemstones. Their feathers appeared to be made of glass, casting colorful shadows across the forest floor. Spears of light shimmered nearby. Dancing orbs hovered in the beams and she realized they weren't just dust motes. They were actual faeries, all whispering about the newcomer who had stepped into their home.

She made her way to the largest grouping of firefly-like beings and asked, "Do you know where I can find the Mountain King?"

All the whispers ceased. The motes floated in a strange, repetitive movement. As if they could convince her they weren't faeries at all.

Sighing, Morgan rolled her eyes. "I know what you are. I've met faeries before."

One orb started drifting away. Nonchalant and so small it

was almost difficult to see, the mote tried to escape the conversation.

Morgan reached out and snatched it from the air. Immediately, the other faeries burst into tiny shouts that sounded like the ringing of bells.

"Put her down, human!"

"That's not yours!"

"Release our sister!"

Morgan was careful not to squish the faerie in her clutches. She held up her closed fist to the other faeries. "This? You want me to let go of this... dust mote?"

"Yes!" they shouted in unison.

"All right, then. Why don't you tell me how to find the Mountain King? I'll let her go in trade for the information."

They all gathered together, hovering like a single orb. They whispered over each other until Morgan couldn't guess what they were saying. Their words were so jumbled, she doubted they even knew what the others were saying.

Faeries.

Morgan waited patiently for them to make their decision. The faerie in her hand tried biting through her palm, but her hands were calloused and leathery from years of labor. The faerie would need much sharper teeth to break free.

Finally, the other faeries settled back into their strange hovering pattern. "First, release our sister."

"No can do," Morgan replied, shaking her head. "I'm not letting go of her until I get my information."

She wasn't stupid. The moment she released the faerie, the others would burst away into flight and she'd get nothing out of them.

They all bunched up again. This time, Morgan let out a long, exasperated sigh. "I don't have all day. I can just crush her and get on with it."

"No!" The faeries shouted. "Fine then. If you keep going straight through the forest, you'll come to the largest tree. Take a left there, and his home is in the clearing. Now release her, demon!"

She opened her hand and let the faerie burst out. "I'm not a demon, just a witch."

"Well whatever you are, you aren't very nice," the faeries muttered and then flew off to wherever they felt safe.

Perhaps they would let the Mountain King know a very "not nice" witch had invaded the forest. Maybe he would come to find her first, although she doubted it. Faeries didn't like to work all that much, and she had a feeling the king would be the worst of them all.

Continuing through the woods, she reached up and shifted branches out of her way. Gently. Ever so gently.

She might be a little rough around the edges with other beings like herself, but plants were special. Growing up, they were the only things she could control. And Morgan had gotten very good at controlling them.

Her gardens always grew out of hand. They produced more vegetables and fruits than any other field in the area. It was the only way she'd known she was a witch.

Others had accused her of magic because her crops were far better than anyone else's. They swore she was casting spells to make everything grow. At the time, Morgan hadn't realized she'd been doing exactly that.

On the way to the largest tree, Morgan stopped and palmed a fern who struggled to grow in the shadows. "Here, little one," she whispered. Breathing out, she gave the tiniest bit of her own life force to the plant. In response, it grew two feet higher. Large enough to soak in the sun's beam.

Would she ever heal a person? Hopefully never. People were cruel and harsh in her experience. Plants weren't judgmental or unkind. They liked a person because they could see into their souls and know if they were pure of heart.

The largest tree in the forest loomed before her. She was shocked at the size of it, though perhaps she shouldn't have been. This was a faerie forest. They knew how to make plants grow better than the greatest of hedge witches.

The tree was the size of a mac truck, and though she tried to stay out of the cities, it reminded her of a skyscraper. So tall it touched the clouds. It was like a god.

Morgan got down onto her knees and bowed low, forehead grazing the ground. "Well met, being of old. Grow strong and may your roots descend into another realm."

The tree shifted, its leaves fluttering in the breeze.

She'd consider that a good omen, even though she had gotten very close to the Mountain King now. She turned to the left and picked her way toward the clearing. The castle should be nearby.

What kind of castle would a green king like this live in? She could only imagine it was something ostentatious. Perfectly manicured and earthy. Perhaps covered in roses, because everyone liked the romance of roses.

The ground rose into a strange, almost mountain like outcropping. Moss covered every inch. She'd have to get down on her hands and knees to clamber up. Breathing hard, Morgan swore as her boots slipped.

She used these boots all the time. They were sturdy, and the heel had always given her purchase. Something in the ground was preventing her from climbing, or at least making it difficult.

"Hands stick and boots level, make this stupid, earthy ground mellow." The remainder of her pinky nail fell off, and she felt one of her teeth loosen.

She hated performing magic when there was nothing else to sacrifice. *This is how witches ended up ugly*, she thought. *Sacrifice something other than yourself.*

The ground flattened. It allowed her to finally climb to the top of the rise where she was certain the castle would appear like a whale from the ocean. It would be too flashy and she'd judge the king even more than she already did.

But no castle rose before her. Instead, the only thing in the valley below was a circular clearing and a small, moss covered hut. Someone who knew what they were doing had laid the simple thatch roof. Moss grew atop it, and none of the grass had rotted.

Stones were placed all around the circle, creating a swirl that started in the center of a small walkway and spread out around the house, through the garden, and out to the edges of the clearing. On all sides, steep hills rose to protect it. Or perhaps keep something deep within.

This was where the Mountain King lived? Surely not. She even shook her head in denial. No faerie king would catch himself dead in such a simple abode.

His right hand must live here, or perhaps the servant who delivered people to the king.

Her mind wrapped around the thought and settled upon it, certain this was the only possible outcome. A faerie king didn't live here.

A sharp thwack echoed through the clearing. She ducked lower, pressing her belly to the moss and waiting for some kind of attack. Another thwack followed the first. Perhaps arrows sinking deep into the trunk of a nearby tree?

But the sound was familiar...

Was someone chopping wood?

She crawled along the rim of the crater or clearing or whatever the faeries called it. The edge was dangerously steep in some places, but finally she saw what was behind the moss covered cottage.

A man stood at the back, chopping wood.

"Oh no," she muttered. "Why'd he have to be handsome?"

This couldn't be anyone but the faerie king. Though the lesser fae were small and adorable, the leaders of the faeries were remarkably human in their beauty. He was at least six and a half feet tall. Long, dark hair reached the middle of his ribs in tangled, sweat stained locks. His back was to her, but impressive muscles flexed as he lifted the axe over his head. Not just back muscles. Strong, bulky muscles along his sides rippled as he brought the axe down.

His pants, an old style that suggested he hadn't been to the human world in a very long time, rode low on his hips. The tops of his round buttocks glistened with sweat and they shouldn't be as attractive as they were. Damn, the man had a downright bitable ass on him.

Oh, how was this fair? She was supposed to kill the man, not drool over him.

Why was she so attracted? Not a clue. She shouldn't have the desire to actually lick a person, but there it was. She wanted to lick those two dimples just above his delicious ass and see what noise he made.

Right. Witch and fae didn't mix, not well at least. She'd seen it a hundred times. Magic like theirs couldn't mingle without explosions happening, usually at the expense of the witch.

Faeries never took responsibility for their actions.

She needed to stop staring at the sweaty faerie king chopping wood, and figure out how she would kill him. The roof didn't extend over his head, so she couldn't pull it down. There was a boulder near him, though. If she could lift it quick enough, she might slam it against his skull.

Either would work, if she was fast. She'd have to untangle her tongue from the roof of her mouth first.

As if that were happening any time soon.

She knew faeries weren't mind readers, but the king stopped what he was doing. Her thoughts hadn't been projected, and she knew she hadn't made a sound. Morgan was tongue-tied, not foolish.

He let the axe fall to his side and shifted his grip into something far more aggressive. He tilted his head, not looking at her but listening. An overgrown beard covered his face.

At least that was something. The Mountain King was also an unkempt mountain man.

That shouldn't have made him even more attractive, but somehow it did.

She stayed frozen in place, waiting for him to either look in her direction or return to chopping wood. He couldn't know she was here, not until she was ready for it.

Morgan sank lower and pressed her face against the moss. Casting another spell would only draw more attention. Besides, she didn't want to lose a tooth just before meeting a king.

She counted to ten and then peered once more over the edge into the clearing. The king had disappeared along with his axe.

"Damn it," she muttered. "Now what am I going to do?"

4

———

He pressed his back against the wall of the cabin, axe held loose between his fingertips. If he had to, he could swing the weapon with enough force to cleave through flesh and bone.

It'd been a long time since he'd seen battle. Many years ago, he'd fought with the fae in the War to End All Wars. The one that had decided whether the magical creatures would hide from the humans, or if they would come out from the shadows.

He hadn't cared. Faeries would continue to live as they desired to live. If they showed themselves, humans wouldn't be frightened of his kind. They would revere them.

But the human hiding on the hill wasn't showing itself. A few humans had stumbled into his realm before. They fell through a stray mushroom circle or even a few standing stones back in the day when those had been more prevalent. The humans always worshiped him as a god.

This one hid. And that meant she was dangerous.

Scales rasped up his arm, coiling around his bicep so his familiar could lift its mouth to his ear, "Liam, I cannot see her anymore."

"That's because we're behind a building," he responded. "You can't see through buildings, Arcane."

The snake hissed long and low, its tongue tickling his ear. "No need to be rude."

His familiar was a strange creature, but one he'd grown rather fond of over the years. The snake had taken many forms in life. Once a boa constrictor. Once a python. These days, he was a small green garden snake. The form suited his purpose well.

Liam kept the snake coiled around his arm most of the time, other than when he cut wood to heat the cabin in the chilly nights. Then he placed the snake on the ground. His familiar had seen the woman at the top of the rise from his perch on the pile of cut logs.

"What did she look like?" Liam murmured, leaning around the corner of the cottage. He couldn't see her just yet, but was certain she'd poke her head up again.

"Black hair," the snake said. "Pale skin. Enormous eyes and strange garb I've never seen before."

"Humans." Liam hated them. Always chopping away at the earth. At this rate, there'd be nothing left in just a few years.

"Terrifying creatures. They're so afraid of snakes they kill them on sight."

Humans killed everything they feared. Insects, snakes, each other. It didn't matter. They fed off bloodshed and violence.

Perhaps this one wanted violence as well. He had to find out. "Did you see a weapon?"

"Oh yes, huge weapon. Lots of danger." The snake tightened around his bicep like a vise, clamping down on the blood flow. "Terrifying."

"What kind of weapon, Arcane?"

The beast hesitated. "I don't know."

Liam closed his eyes in frustration and reminded himself he liked Arcane. The creature was even his best friend, if he was giving away titles. Killing him for being dramatic would only land Liam back in solitary confinement. "Did she, or did she not have a weapon?"

"I didn't see one, but I'm certain she is dangerous."

Right. So the snake had decided the human was scary. Therefore, she must have a weapon. Because that made sense.

Liam reached up and unraveled the snake from around his arm. Carefully, he set Arcane down into the grass. "Find her, familiar of mine."

"What?" Arcane hissed. "You'd have me risk my life? Why?"

"To save mine. If the human wishes to harm me, then she is a threat I will remove. But I won't attack her without knowing what she wants first." He nudged the snake with his foot. "Now, off with you. Find her and see what nonsense she's up to before I use the axe on you."

Arcane hissed out a long complaint, but slithered off into the grass until Liam could no longer see him. The familiar was loyal, if he was anything. Cowardly and dramatic, but loyal.

In the meantime, Liam intended on returning to what he did best.

Green magic.

He reached behind him and laid his palm against the side of the cottage. With a heavy sigh, the building split down the wall, allowing him access through the wood which had once been whole. He slipped through the new opening and sealed it once he was through.

The rooms beyond were quaint, simple, and filled to the brim with as many plants as he could fit indoors. A small seating area to his left was the only place to relax in the living room. Every other nook was filled with plants needing special help.

The other faerie kings were more inclined to live in lavish spaces with lots of room. Liam had to pick through the clustered pots, each of differing sizes, crowding every inch of free space on his floor. Someday the plants would go back outside where they belonged.

But for now, he wanted to make sure they were close at hand. Just in case they needed him.

Liam made his way back to the very end of the house. He kept most of the large plants here, and perhaps the most important one of all.

His monstera had grown far beyond the size she should have. She took up an entire wall with her leaves larger than he was tall. The humans called her a "swiss cheese" plant because of the holed pattern in her leaves. He thought it was rather insulting to call something so beautiful "cheese".

"Hello, my lovely," he breathed, closing the door behind him with a soft click. "I was wondering if you might help me."

The plant moved as though a wind had stirred her leaves. With no windows in this room, he knew it was her happiness at his presence.

Her emotions were always a breath of fresh air in this place where he always felt so alone. She was more than a friend. She was family.

Liam picked his way past pots filled with sunburnt english ivy and rubber plants until he stood before his beautiful monstera. He pet one of her largest leaves, holding her against his side. "There's a stranger in the forest. Did you know?"

Her voice whispered to life in his ear. Deep and vibrating with power, "I have spoken with the trees. They have seen her."

Strange. The trees weren't friendly to strangers, and if she had walked through the ones Monstera could speak with, then she had come by portal.

"Faerie made?" he asked.

"Yes," Monstera replied. "They said she walked through a portal activated by faerie blood."

He stroked a hand down her rubbery leaf. "But she's

human. Arcane could smell her on the wind. How could she open a portal with faerie blood?"

Unless she had sacrificed a faerie, as humans were wont to do. He'd seen them do worse things to his kind. And gaining an audience with the Mountain King?

A human would do anything for that.

Monstera shuddered. "She had no blood on her when she arrived. They do not believe she harmed one of your kind to come here."

"The trees put their faith in her innocence?" Somehow everything got even more confusing. His most trusted guardians would allow her into their realm without complaint?

He continued to stroke her leaf wrapped around his waist. Monstera tried to reassure him in the only way she knew how. By letting him hold on to her and breathe in the scent of earth and growing things.

"How are you feeling?" Monstera asked. "You were... not yourself a few days ago."

A flash of memory burned in his mind. He didn't want to think about losing his temper the other day. How he'd been so angry he couldn't think of anything other than power and greed and anger.

He'd awoken stuck to the wall. Vines growing in his hair and bark roughening his skin.

"A momentary lapse," he replied. "I lost my head for a few moments. It won't happen again."

"Won't it?" Monstera shook, her great leaves shuddering in his arms. "You know what happens if you continue to deny your destiny."

Destiny. The word haunted his every step. When he was young, people wanted him to grow up and follow the path of a faerie king. He'd done that. Then they wanted him to become more powerful. So he had accepted the overwhelming amount of power his station required. Now, they wanted him to take an ancient throne that brought about the end of the world.

He knew how dangerous such a path could be. He knew how dark his soul would become if he sat upon that throne.

But with it also came responsibility. The world would change for the better. He agreed with the fae that humanity had destroyed too much. Yet, he wouldn't be able to hide in this realm of his own making with creatures of his own choice. He wouldn't grow plants in his home and breathe life into them individually.

The throne, though good for the world, was the end of life as he knew it.

He released his hold on Monstera's leaf. She settled back into the position she found most comfortable and waited.

"I promise," he said. "Everything will work out the way it should. Destiny or no. But first, I need your help."

Before he wasted another thought on such royal matters, he had a wayward human to deal with.

5
____

Morgan didn't know how long she waited on the rise. She counted to three hundred before she gave up and finally lifted her head. The man still hadn't come out from wherever he'd gone.

At first, she thought the faerie king would come for her. She listened to the forest, waiting for the sound of a footstep or even the crackle of magic. If he had known she was on the rise, then he would approach.

Faeries were territorial. The king would want her off his land as swiftly as possible. Which meant he would strike, pin her to the ground, and then force her to leave. Right?

When none of that happened, Morgan braced herself on her forearm and blew a sharp breath at the hair in her face. "Well," she muttered. "I guess it's time for me to meet the king."

He couldn't hide from her, and now that she'd botched this initial meeting, she had to try different tactics. No one wanted to be seduced by the woman who trespassed. But also no king lived in a cabin in the woods. So much for waltzing into court and playing the sultry temptress.

Scrambling to her feet, she made her way down into the

clearing. Every step was treacherous, but this time the ground didn't fight against her.

Her boots kept her stable and surefooted. She held her arms out to the sides, fists clenched with magic tingling between her fingers.

She would make sacrifices if he attacked. But a shield was no simple spell. Or rather, it *was* a simple spell, but it came at a great price.

Morgan would very much like to keep all the hair on her head.

She skidded to a stop in the clearing and paused. No sounds echoed through it, not even the song of the birds. They had sang so prettily before the king sensed her presence.

Some assassin she was. The first time she saw her prey, he'd run from her like a gazelle from a lion.

Oh, she quite liked that image. Baring her teeth, she stalked toward the cabin with single minded intent. It was time to catch a king.

She rounded the back and approached the front door. Even that was simple in this strange little hut in the middle of nowhere. Just a regular wood door. No window, no glass, no markings. Just oak with a wrought iron bar as a handle.

Could he not lock it? Strange. She would have thought a king would at least have a lock on his door.

Curiouser and curiouser. Somehow she felt as though she were going down Alice's rabbit hole.

Morgan stepped onto the path to his home. The grass at the base of the door shifted and then a small garden snake reared up, mouth open and hissing at her.

She lifted a single brow. "Just what do you think you're doing?"

Now, she didn't expect the snake to respond. But she should have guessed it might. She was, after all, on faerie lands.

The garden snake hissed again, "You are not welcome here. State your reason for being."

She let out a soft snort before she caught herself. "Uh, existing to annoy creatures like you, I suppose."

The snake snapped its mouth closed. If it could furrow its brows, it seemed to do so now as it stared back at her in confusion. "Pardon?"

"You asked what my reason for being was." She shrugged. "I supposed it's always been to annoy."

"I don't-"

"Understand?" Morgan interrupted the creature because, frankly, she didn't have time for conversations with a snake. "That's all right. I need to go inside the cottage now, so please slither aside."

It straightened at her order and bared tiny teeth. "I will not! The master wishes to be alone, and you will not disturb him."

"And you're the one he sent to stop me?" This time she laughed. Cruel it might be, but the snake was the length of her forearm. Not to mention, garden snakes weren't poisonous.

The snake tried to make itself even larger. "My name is Arcane! I am the familiar of the Mountain King, son of the Earth, and Commander of green magic. You will not laugh at me!"

"My greatest apologies if I insulted you, Arcane the familiar." She leaned down, pinched her fingers just underneath his jaw, and lifted him into the air. "But you won't stop me. Besides, I thought only witches had familiars?"

Hissing and spitting curses at her, the snake whipped its tail in her grip. He clearly wanted to bite her, mouth opening and closing with urgency. Considering her grip on his hinged jaw, he couldn't do anything but wiggle in her grasp.

"Hold that thought," she muttered, reaching for the door handle. "I'm sure your master will want to hear all your opinions on my fidelity or birthright."

She grabbed onto the iron bar, only to feel magic pulse through her body as though she'd touched a live wire. She dropped the snake. The poor thing didn't need any residual magic coursing through it simply because its master was a fool.

Magic like that shouldn't be in doors, damn it! Had he no sense at all?

Gritting her teeth through the pain, she closed her fingers more firmly around the iron. "You must do better than that," she ground through her teeth.

Perhaps it wasn't the smartest of threats to snarl at a faerie king. The magic surged through her body. She lost her grip on the door and the power sent her flying backwards ten feet. She landed hard on her back. All the breath squeezed from her lungs at the impact and her ribs ached.

Stones pressed against every inch of her body, as if they too were attacking her. The grass blades were sharp against her hands and the back of her neck.

Was he using the earth against her?

She rose onto her elbows, staring at the door and breathing hard. He used green magic against a hedge witch?

Anger made her power spark at her fingertips. If he wanted to play that game, then she'd play the witch card.

The grass was good enough for a sacrifice. She left handprints of dead earth as she pushed herself upright. Each footstep left a mark in his well watered soil, a black smudge of darkness approaching his cottage.

Let the faerie king feel fear. He should quake behind the door wondering what kind of creature had walked into his made-up realm.

She lifted her hands, power crackling between her fingertips. The visible magic looked vaguely like lightning arcing between her fingertips, although it was a lovely shade of pale green.

Morgan focused on the door and directed all her energy

toward it. No incantation was necessary to release the snapping energy, sending it hurtling forward.

The lightning struck the wood and blasted right through it. Energy took the door right off its hinges, sending it three feet into the cottage before it fell with a giant bang. What Morgan hadn't expected were a hundred clay pots filled with plants on the other side.

The wood struck the ground with a sound like a canon, and the following shatter of wood-fired clay was the ratta-tat-tat of a gun.

She flinched. That might have been a little aggressive, and he definitely knew she was attacking him. It might have been smarter to sneak in rather than break down his door like a troll. So much for seducing him.

Morgan stepped onto the broken door and into the room. Shattered clay crunched underneath her heels, and she felt a moment of sadness for the plants upended on the ground. Or worse, crushed under the weight of the wood.

"Sorry," she whispered. "I'll fix you once I'm done with him."

A door at the back of the small cottage opened. She would have sworn a mere wind pushed it open, only to lock eyes with the bearded man beyond. Every inch of him revealed was just as lovely as she feared.

From a distance, the man was attractive. Pleasant to look at and without a doubt fit. All faeries were, however, so that was nothing unexpected.

But this close? The faerie was too much to look at.

His shoulders were broad and still glistening with cooling sweat. His abs were perfectly chiseled, although she didn't know how it was possible for them to look so much like a washboard. And even worse, the muscles over his hips created a perfect "v" dipping into the waistline of his Victorian era trousers.

Damn, he would be difficult to kill.

Long, tangled brown hair fell in front of his eyes, concealing what color they were but not quite hiding the rage pouring off his body. His unkempt beard stuck to his chest, and in his hand, he gripped an axe.

She could have sworn she saw that leaning against the side of the building. Where had he gotten another one? Did he just keep them lying around for the moment a wayward witch wandered into his home?

"Who are you?" he snarled.

"Does it matter?" Morgan didn't think telling a faerie her name was smart, anyway. They knew how to use names to control and the old ways were still strong.

"It very much matters who you are, woman." He took a menacing step closer and tightened his grip around the long handle of the axe.

Careful, she reminded herself. *He's still a faerie and they love their tricks.*

She could only imagine what he could do with that axe. Let alone magic.

As the Mountain King, he had to have one of the greener magics as far as faeries went. That could translate into talking with plants, making things grow, or forcing mountains to move at his bidding. Perhaps even all of those.

Morgan widened her stance, preparing herself for a battle. She held her hands out to the side, fingers relaxed and power bubbling beneath the surface of her skin. "You won't need to know anyone's name where you're going."

He arched a brow and tilted his head. His hair shifted to the side, revealing more of the chiseled face beyond the waterfall of chocolate color. "Have you come here to kill me, human?"

"I have."

"Better people than you have tried, and they always failed."

"Perhaps they did." Morgan took a deep breath and

centered herself. The well of magic deep in her breast stilled its bubbling into a smooth, glass-like surface in her mind. It was ready and so was she. "But no one like me has ever attacked you."

Talking had no purpose when the man was about to be foaming at the mouth. Morgan reached for all the plants around her and pulled hard at the life force growing in their roots. She didn't kill them, not yet. She didn't want to feel anything else die unless she had to.

With a swift flick of her fingers, she sent crackling balls of energy shooting toward him. He side-stepped her attack and twin holes burst through his wall.

The faerie stared at the holes in shock before his wide-eyed gaze met hers. "You're a witch," he said accusingly.

"I am," she replied. Without hesitation, she pulled from the surrounding land again. This time, she was smarter. No more energy he could dodge. Instead, she pushed the magic into the ground.

The earth underneath the floorboards rolled. Wood cracked underneath their feet and sent the remaining pots whirling as she tossed aside them. The faerie slapped his hand against the wall to steady himself.

She'd turned the floor into the waves of the ocean. Her only advantage was she knew where and when the waves would occur.

He didn't.

Morgan scurried to the side of the room where she could see a wall of darts hanging. Once, her mother had told her about such things.

Faerie darts weren't real, even though the legends claimed faeries used them to their advantage. They didn't. Darts were only made by trolls, who gathered magic dust deep in their mines. Once they hit a target, the affected person would fall into a deep sleep.

She wouldn't mind fighting the faerie fair and square. But if he was asleep, he sure would be easier to kill.

Thunderous footsteps approached. She didn't want to distract herself, but Morgan couldn't stop her head from turning and staring over her shoulder.

The faerie ran like he was part bull. The ground threw him off, but he righted himself every time it caught his leg and sent him stumbling in the wrong direction. Grunting, he widened his steps and charged forward.

"Damn it," she muttered, changing course and giving up on the darts. Morgan bolted to the other side of the room and tugged on the plant life harder. She widened the stretch of her magic.

This time, when she pulled on a life force nearby, she heard an answering scream. It split through her skull like he'd hit her with the axe.

The distraction was just enough for the faerie king to get the slip on her. One second, he was a safe distance away at the other side of the room, then the next he was standing in front of her.

Morgan gasped, "Teleportation?"

His tangled beard parted and revealed a blinding smile. "Faeries are capable of far more than that, witch. But you won't know for much longer."

Like lighting, his hand snapped out and grabbed her neck.

If he thought that would kill her, he had another thing coming. Snarling, she grabbed his wrist with her hand and poured all her power into his skin. Bone deep and soul shattering, the witch magic would course through his body like poison.

He tried to fight through it. She gave him credit for his stamina. His hand tightened painfully around her throat and he bared his teeth in a snarl as he tried to overcome the sudden pain in his body.

No one had ever suffered through witch magic. Morgan only had so much power, but enough so they would remain at a standstill until one of them let go.

She would not be the first. He had his hand around her throat. This was life or death. If she let go, he'd kill her. If she didn't let go, then she might still die, but at least she had a fighting chance.

The faerie king cursed and released his hold. The axe dropped onto the floor with a clatter. He stumbled back while clutching his wrist. A bright green handprint glowed where she'd held him.

"Serves you right," she snapped. "You should know better than to grab a witch."

"What infernal magic did you put in me?"

"Infernal?" The laugh shaking her shoulders wasn't a pleasant sound. It was the ancient call of a thousand women who had burned at the stake and a million faeries who never helped them. "Oh, because borrowed magic is all infernal to your kind."

The floor rolled under his feet, sending him tumbling further from her. "That magic is not yours to use."

"No magic is anyone's to use. You faeries have never understood that."

"I can use whatever magic is gifted to me!" he shouted. "Your magic always comes with a price. Faerie magic is free to use and to give."

She scoffed. "That's so like a faerie. You think none of your magic has a price? Witches have paid your price for centuries. A faerie uses magic to take a baby and flames lick a witch's ankles. A faerie heals human crops, and a witch pays with rope burn around her neck. You want to tell me your magic is free? Try a better lie, faerie."

The rolling floor sent him to the ground. He knelt, one knee on the shattered planks, still holding his wrist. A faerie king on his knees before her. What a strange way to end her day.

"Do you want me to apologize?" he asked. His eyes were painfully green. They looked like rolling emerald hills and glowed with so much magic it overwhelmed her senses.

Fresh cut grass teased her nose and the taste of rose petals burst on her tongue. She could hear leaves rustling in the breeze and feel autumn crunching beneath her feet. Green magic unfurled, growing all around her. It filled the roots of every plant, large and small.

The roots underneath her feet were visible, somehow. She could see them all tangling and reaching deep into the ground. They glowed bright green and strong in this place, all of it reaching back to the Mountain King. He was the source of their power.

Every plant in this hidden realm drew from him, sipping at his magic like he was a well deserved rain. He fed them from his life force.

A particular root caught her attention, long and thick. It pulsed with glimmering verdant energy. Small sparks seemed to shower off it, all leading back to the Mountain King in the center of the room. Like an umbilical cord.

Morgan's gaze found him again. Her eyes locked on his hand pressed against the floor, which wasn't rolling anymore. It wasn't even moving. How was he doing that?

Dust motes floated just above her head, like pollen, except it wasn't pollen at all. Her lungs breathed in air, but she didn't want that air in her body. It was contaminated. She could see his power, but she couldn't stop breathing it in.

The room warped. The walls shimmered with sparkling green lights and the floor was rivers of roots all flowing back to him. To the man in the center of the room with his palm pressed against the revealed earth.

"What are you doing to me?" she murmured. Her voice

didn't sound like her own. Her tongue was too thick to form words she'd said a hundred times before.

"Sleep, witch," he growled. His voice was a lullaby. So lovely to listen to and she wanted to sleep.

She hadn't slept in so long. Nightmares plagued her rest. She dreamed in painful memories of dark things reaching for her in the night. Things she shouldn't know about people whose minds weren't locked away.

No, Morgan thought. *He can't know.*

"What can't I know?" the Mountain King asked.

"I will never tell you my secrets." Morgan slurred the words at him. "Faeries should all burn as witches have burned for centuries."

He tucked a finger underneath her chin and tilted her head up. When had he moved? She thought he was still in the center of the room, yet he was here.

Heat spread from the single touch. Her entire body reacted to just the smallest of pets. Morgan arched toward him, seeking that green magic like a heat missile. But it wasn't green magic making her stomach tighten and her heart race.

The Mountain King grinned. "So you're mad at faeries because you blame us for all the witches who have died? Is that it?"

She would have spat in his face if her body would listen. But it wasn't under her control anymore.

It was under his.

He tsked. "You should never have tried to attack a faerie. Let alone a faerie king. Sleep now."

Morgan watched his hand descend and pass over her eyes. Then she knew nothing but darkness.

6

———

Liam sat on the remains of a pot he'd flipped upside down. He braced his forearms against his knees and pressed steepled fingers against his lips.

A witch. Here.

When had witches discovered how to infiltrate faerie realms? He'd hidden this place well. The surrounding shields were still strong, he'd checked the moment she'd fallen asleep.

No one should have been able to enter his home without faerie blood. The trees assured him there had been no blood on her when she entered. Unless she was a particularly savvy witch, and he doubted she was, she'd gotten into his home without violence.

This led to an even darker thought.

Had a faerie betrayed him?

He stared at the woman wrapped in Monstera's leaves. The large plant had insisted upon creating a prison for the witch who attacked him. Now, the woman rested within the large fronds wrapped around her like a straightjacket.

The witch was still asleep. He wouldn't wake her until he

had some course of action. Unfortunately, that was proving to be rather difficult with a creature like this.

Her magic was extremely powerful. If they'd been in the human realm, her trick with the waves might not have been so impressive. However, this entire place was his own creation. The floor wasn't a floor, but magic and illusion.

And she had warped his magic into something of her own.

Liam had never heard of a witch with power like that.

Scales rasped through the remains of their fight. Arcane made his way to Liam's side. A pot clanged as the snake knocked it over. "Master?"

"What is it?"

Arcane reared up beside him and stared at the woman. "She's a witch."

"I'm aware."

"A very powerful witch."

He sighed. "Yes, I believe you are correct. I've seen her magic myself."

Liam didn't want to think about the work required to fix the aftermath of their fight. The pots were shattered. A hundred plants moaned in his mind, but he didn't have the time to fix their ailments. Or the power. This little witch had drained him faster than any other opponent, and he'd fought in the faerie wars.

Faerie dust covered the room in a fine layer of green. He'd seen her reaching for the darts, their pink tips covered in troll dust. The woman had wanted him to fall asleep and not wake back up. Smart, but also foolish when her intention was so clear.

Where had she learned how to fight?

He had a thousand and one questions, but none he'd answer while she still slept.

Sighing, Liam looked down at Arcane. "I'm going to wake her up. Are you sure you want to be here for this?"

Arcane straightened his spine even more and bared his fangs. "She picked me up and threw me into the tomatoes. I want answers."

That shouldn't have been so funny, but Liam found himself silencing a chuckle. Few people had the courage to pick up a faerie familiar. Let alone one who was hundreds of years old and had been every form of snake imaginable.

The woman had tossed Arcane into the vegetables. He bit his lip at the image.

Balls. The woman definitely had balls.

"All right, Monstera," he said. "Hold on to her tight. We don't trust her yet."

"Of course, Master."

He snapped his fingers and all the faerie dust in the room disappeared.

The woman blinked her eyes open. It took a while, as it always did with humans. Her eyes narrowed the moment they focused, then she struggled against her bindings.

Monstera tightened her man-sized leaves. He could hear the telltale creak of bones, and the witch stopped moving.

She breathed shallowly. "Tell your plant to ease up."

"I don't think I will." He remained seated and relaxed, but he wanted to fly at her and end it all. Too bad he had questions for the witch. "Why don't you tell me who you are now?"

"I'm not telling you anything."

Liam lifted a brow and Monstera squeezed a little more. The breath wheezed out of the witch's lungs. Her eyes widened as she realized she couldn't inhale while the plant held her so tightly.

To her credit, she lasted until her face was purple. Only then did she nod at him.

Monstera eased up enough for the woman to fill her lungs with air. And while she got herself back under at least some semblance of control, Liam surveyed her.

Though he didn't want to think good of the witch, she was beautiful. Her dark hair glistened in the dim light. Her eyes were a startling shade of hazel, blazing green with power. He hadn't thought humans could have green magic. This one surprised him more and more just by existing.

He'd been alone too long. Liam noticed her soft curves too much. The swells of her breasts were nearly as tantalizing as the curve of her hips.

Monstera's leaves left the woman's clothing askew. The leather of her pants couldn't shift, but the billowing white shirt had ridden up to reveal a waist so pale he could have traced the webbing of blue veins underneath her skin.

He couldn't afford to think like this. She was the enemy. She was a witch who had come into his home to kill him, and that should have been enough to kill her.

And yet, it wasn't.

He leaned back, straightened his spine and rose to his fullest height. "Are you going to tell me who you are, now?"

"I'm a witch," she snapped.

"Clearly."

He didn't want to force Monstera to squeeze the woman again, but he would. The plant was all too happy to remind the witch who was in control.

The leaves tightened before the woman let out a snarl. "Fine! My name is Morgan Lefair, I was hired to kill you."

Liam lifted a brow again. "Yes, that much is clear. I don't care what your name is, woman."

"Don't faeries collect names like gemstones?" she asked. "Every one of you wants to control someone or something whenever you want. My name is more powerful on your tongue than any spell."

He supposed she was right. Most faeries needed a name to control humans. "I'm not just a faerie. I'm the Mountain King. I don't need your name to control you."

He could boil her blood because there was metal in her. He could twist her form because carbon existed in the human body. There were so many things he could do and he didn't need permission to use her name.

Liam wouldn't, though. He had never found humans to be a challenge, therefore, he ignored their existence. He just wanted to be left alone.

Arcane slithered closer to the woman. "Why do they want to kill the Mountain King?"

Ah yes, he should have asked that. Liam didn't care if someone wanted to kill him. Someone always did. Faerie kings weren't exactly liked by any kind of creature. He was more concerned about her abilities to carry out the deed.

He'd never worried someone might actually kill him before. Not until her.

The woman, Morgan, he reminded himself, relaxed against Monstera. "I don't know why they want to kill him."

He could sense the lie long before she even said the words.

Arcane's tongue flicked out and Liam knew the creature was tasting for deception. It was one of the best tricks his familiar knew how to do. One Liam had taught him.

The snake weaved in the air, back and forth like a cobra in a basket. "You're lying, human."

"I'm not lying."

"Yes, you are. I can taste it like whiskey in the air. Bitter and tempting for all humans. Why is it that your kind finds lying so entertaining? Why lie when you could tell the truth?"

Her face paled even more, if that was possible. Morgan licked her lips, and his gaze caught on the glimpse of a pink tongue.

So pretty. He'd always loved pink things. Flowers, pale silk ribbons, the blush of a woman as it spread across her chest.

He'd been alone for too long. Clearly. Lusting after the witch sent to kill him was a new low.

Liam crossed his legs, uncrossed them at the sudden discomfort, then looked around for his escape. He couldn't be in this room with her a moment longer when all he could think about was that pink tongue.

What could she do with it? Faeries were uninhibited people. They used their bodies like musical instruments. Humans were a different matter. He'd only taken a few of them to bed and they were always so deliciously shy.

He didn't think this witch had a shy bone in her body. She struck him as the kind of creature to take charge, a woman who knew what she wanted and how to take it.

What would she take from him?

He stood abruptly. The snake stopped moving and stared over his non-existent shoulder while the woman glared.

Liam wanted to tell her to stop frowning. All he could think about was how close that expression was to the one she might make while screaming his name, and damn it. He needed to go.

He growled, "Get out of my realm, human."

"I'll just go back through the portal then." She struggled against Monstera again, but this time the plant didn't know if she should stop the witch.

He didn't care how she left, only that she was gone by the time he returned. Stalking away from the room, he paused at the door when her words flickered to life in his mind.

The portal?

So someone had let her into his realm. A faerie *had* betrayed him and sent someone to kill their king.

Portals were rare. He knew all the portals and where they were because he'd built them himself. The Mountain King should know when someone waltzed into his home. A tingle of magic had always warned him when someone was approaching.

But he hadn't felt the tingle. Maybe he'd been so engrossed in his work he hadn't noticed, but such a slip wasn't like him.

Liam turned back to the woman, dread churning in his stomach. "Where is this portal?"

The witch stopped struggling against the leaves. She stared at him with her mouth agape, as though he'd asked her to come to bed with him. "In the trees," she replied. "Near the dust faeries."

There were no portals near the dust faeries. Not a single one, because they liked to chatter at visitors about things they shouldn't know. His worst dreams had been realized.

Someone *had* opened a portal, without permission, and sent a human through to kill him. They'd spilled faerie blood. Blood only meant to be used when a faerie was in mortal danger.

Clearing his throat, Liam leaned against the door jamb and crossed his arms. He stared at the woman as he pawed through his thoughts.

She couldn't stay. His reaction to her was frightening and strong. If she stayed, he'd do something he regretted and then letting her go would be even more difficult. She was right that faeries liked to collect gemstones, and she was the most precious he'd seen in a long time.

But she also knew a rebel faerie. She knew why they wanted him dead. He could still smell the lie radiating off her like rotting meat. And the witch was capable of green magic, stronger than any he'd ever seen before.

Another question he needed answered. It seemed this woman was full of impossible things and he couldn't let her go until he knew the meaning to each and every one of them.

Faeries couldn't lie. The spell surrounding his people enchained his tongue as well. But he could twist the truth at least a little, and perhaps the woman would make her own assumptions.

"The portals only open on Imbolc and Samhain," he replied.

It wasn't a lie. He had omitted the information that the portals opened on those days to all neighboring kingdoms and humans. They didn't need permission to pass into his land for the feasts and festivities.

Portals were, technically, always open. He just knew when people were coming and going from them on the other days.

Let her make her own assumptions.

Her eyes widened in shock and he knew she'd made the correct leap in her mind. The one that would let him control her for a little while longer.

"What?" she whispered. Her shocked horror spread through the room as green magic leaked out of her. He could see it dripping from her body and landing back into the earth in wet plops.

When had humans gotten so strong?

"Faerie," her snarl echoed. "Tell me truth. I need to go home and if I can't kill you, then I'll gladly go with my tail tucked between my legs."

There were many things he wanted to do between her legs, and none of them had to do with a tail. Liam shook himself clear of the thought and left the room before he did something he regretted.

Her voice followed him as she shouted, "Faerie! I will destroy you for this!"

Faerie courts help him, but he hoped she did. What a way to go.

7

———

What was she going to do? Her herbs, her home, her job. Everything was back in the human realm and she couldn't leave them for more than a few days. Let alone...

Morgan froze. She'd be late to the witches summit. Or worse, she would miss her own coven meeting.

They'd kill her. Any witch who didn't pledge fealty to the others, the ones who were deemed outcasts, were too dangerous to allow alone in the woods.

They'd hunt her just like the other magical creatures. If she missed the summit, she might as well give up her life here and now. They wouldn't stop until she was dead, and her bones burned.

Plenty of witches wanted to wield the torch. They didn't like hedge witches anymore than they liked kitchen witches. They thought her weak and a grim omen for the name of power.

She was so dead.

Morgan berated herself for ever taking this job. She should have known the faerie king would ruin her plans. Faeries always did.

The snake at her feet shifted. The creature had stared at the door for a long time before it must have finally realized its master wasn't returning.

It turned to glare at her. "Well, what am I supposed to do with you?" the snake hissed.

"Let me go?" she replied.

"I can let you go, but you won't like what happens next." The creature's long body coiled in a slithering circle.

"Oh?"

If a snake could grin, the creature managed it. "I'll eat you."

Morgan couldn't help it. She burst out laughing until her entire body ached. "A garden snake? Eating me?" Her shoulders shook, and her ribs protested the hysterical sounds erupting from her body. "Maybe a finger or a toe, but I don't think you'd have much luck!"

Her mirth spread, shaking the plant until she realized the monstera holding her was laughing, too. If she listened hard enough, feminine chuckles spread through the roots.

The snake hissed out a long, angry sound before it settled onto the ground and slithered to the door. "Both of you have no respect. No respect!"

She supposed she didn't, but how was she to respect a creature that small with so much bluster? The snake was adorable and loyal to its master. But it was still just a garden snake with the heart of a boa.

When she was alone with the monstera, Morgan reached deep into her power. The well of magic she'd always envisioned as a pool was dreadfully low. She could see the bottom and wade through it up to her mind's knees, but only that.

She dipped her fingers into it, then used a few drops to ask, "Can you let me go? Or does your master wish me to be held like this forever?"

In response, the monstera unfurled its great leaves.

"Thank you," Morgan said as it helped her onto her feet. "You're very strong."

The monstera then did something Morgan didn't expect. The plant shifted, and she could hear a voice in her head. "Thank you, witch. Your magic is very strong."

A small sound of surprise escaped her lips before she could catch it. The little scoff wasn't meant as an insult, but a sound of shock that a plant was... talking. Like this. So easily when it should have required magic poured into it.

Perhaps that was the miracle of this place. The man who owned it, who'd clearly created the entire realm, had fed more magic into the soil than Morgan had thought possible.

She placed a hand against her aching ribs and forced her body into a low bow. Though it hurt, the monstera deserved what little respect she could afford. "It's an honor to meet you. What shall I call you?"

"Monstera is the name the Mountain King gave me."

"That's not a name. It's your species."

"And it is also what he calls me."

The argument was over before it had begun. The plant had no intention of ever letting Morgan sway her thoughts on the Mountain King. Likely to his own benefit, considering the creature wasn't going anywhere. And it had more importance to him than the others.

Morgan would have to be blind to not see Monstera was the Mountain King's favorite. He'd given her a place of honor in the house, along with the sick plants in the other room. Morgan could feel them dying, too far gone for her magic to help.

"Did he make all this?" she asked, hesitant to know the answer but needing the truth. "Not just the cottage but the realm and the plants?"

"He cannot create life from nothing, if that's what you're asking. But yes, he has fed all of us. We call him life."

The Mountain King had created a new realm for himself so

he could escape the actual world. Then, he'd brought plants from everywhere he could and fed them his own life force, his own magic.

Which meant when she had pulled from the land, she'd actually pulled from him.

Morgan looked down at her hands and felt ill. The power in her was his. She'd taken from a faerie and used their own magic against them. Such an act felt as though she had somehow desecrated him and herself without knowing.

"If I can't go home, I can't imagine I'm welcome to stay here. I tried to kill him."

Monstera's leaves shook. "And a valiant attempt it was. There are guest houses outside, just beyond the ridge. The grass will take you there."

The grass?

Morgan tried hard not to ask questions. She knew the faerie realms were different and if the plants of this place were feeding off their master, then they could do unimaginable things.

Blades of grass could change forms into switchblades. Flowers could open up into eyes.

No place was safe here for her.

Why in the world had that stupid vampire thought she could come in here and kill the king with no issues at all?

Why had she thought she could do this on her own?

Sighing, Morgan nodded at Monstera. "Thank you. For what it's worth, I'm not sure I'll try to kill him again."

"You'd be foolish to try, but I don't think you give up easily either."

How sweet of the plant to think Morgan was so capable. The handsome faerie had slapped her down like a cat playing with a mouse. She knew when the noose threatened. Any wrong step would put her deep below the ground with his roots tangled in her hair.

Her self preservation was much stronger than her need to stay out of a magical jail. Morgan would rather run for the rest of her life.

If Morgan wanted more magic, and she did, then she'd need to find something else to fill her well. She could sacrifice pieces of herself, but that would only make things worse. Drawing from the earth here was only drawing from him. He'd feel it. Thus, that could not happen.

"Stuck between a rock and a hard place," she muttered.

The rock being her own lack of magic. The hard place being... well. Him.

She'd seen his discomfort when he watched her with that heated gaze. A man couldn't hide such an impressive bulge just by placing his hands over his lap. What she didn't understand was why the faerie king had tried to hide his reaction to her tied up body, when he could have acted on it. Faeries weren't known for their self restraint.

She crunched over the broken pots and the door so she could make her way outside. The cottage looked like a war zone. Between the two of them, their magic had burst quite a few of the windows and ruined his floor.

She wouldn't apologize for the destruction. He had started the entire battle, if only he'd laid down and died a little easier, she would have left without a peep.

Although, the portals made leaving a little harder.

That damned Aster should have told her she'd be stuck here for a season. The Celtic festivals made sense, considering faeries still valued the old ways. But what if she had killed the faerie king?

She couldn't have gone home with no explanation. Alone. With all his creatures and plants angry that she'd just starved them to death.

Morgan glowered down at the grass and opened her arms wide. "Well? You're supposed to be taking me somewhere to sleep. Preferably somewhere far away from the faerie king with all his tangled, dreadlocked hair and that ridiculous beard."

At least she could focus on the nasty things. He was unkempt. Dirty. He'd smelled like earth, loam, and man sweat.

Men were disgusting creatures. Wild men were even worse. He couldn't tempt her with his beautiful body and faerie magic.

All that power in a body like that...

"Stop it," she muttered. "Enough is enough, Morgan. You can get some sleep, sacrifice a few fingernails, maybe a few teeth, and then figure out what you're doing in the morning."

Getting home was her first priority. She needed to find whatever portal was still working and then beg its guardian to let her through. And if there wasn't a guardian, then... A blank space in her mind existed where a plan should have been.

Either way, she couldn't keep standing in the middle of his garden like a giant dolt. She had to get moving.

The grass next to her right foot parted. Almost like someone had brushed it aside with a comb. A long line led away from the cottage toward the opposite rise.

"Ah, I assume that's the path?" she asked.

The grass said nothing in response. Maybe this was one plant here who couldn't talk.

She strode away from the cottage with measured steps, even though she wanted to run. Morgan would have liked nothing more than to sprint in a random direction. Far away from this place.

Whatever it took to make her feel as though she didn't still have a piece of him in her.

The sun set on the horizon before she reached her destination. A guest room, the Monstera had said. Or something similar to that.

Faeries weren't the cottage types. She was surprised the king stayed in the cabin, but perhaps the grass was bringing her to the proper castle. Maybe she'd just caught him at a bad time.

The sun dipped low enough on the horizon, and darkness swept through the forest. The grass changed its guidance. Instead of parting like hair, it gripped her feet. Every few moments she'd feel the ground become sticky. The grass would wrap around her boots and tug, shifting her direction without her having to see it.

Useful, but terrifying.

"Please tell me it's close," she said. Even for a green witch, grass doing all this was unnerving.

Plants shouldn't move on their own unless she told them to. But these plants all had a mind of their own and were more than happy to prove it.

Whatever the king had done to them, they had powers unlike anything she'd seen before. Powers no plant should have. Powers only people should have.

Finally, the grass stopped tugging at her. Glowing white lights bounced in the distance. Orbs dancing where she must be staying.

"Thank you," she said.

Her mother had always said politeness was the most important thing in a faerie realm. If one was helped, thank them. Otherwise, she would owe the faeries a debt, and no one wanted to owe a faerie debt.

She picked her way over fallen logs and through the trees. A small room had been created out of vines and bent tree limbs. The bed was made of moss and soft peat. Vines trailed down from nearby trees and created walls around the small nest. A pillow of autumn leaves waited for her head.

It was lovely, but it was not a bed.

"I suppose I shouldn't have expected more from faeries," she whispered.

"More?" his voice erupted from the shadows. "Is this not suitable for your needs?"

Morgan froze. She could feel the vibrations of his voice like a physical touch down her spine. As if he'd touched her. As if..

The king reached out and placed a hand against the small of her back. He was so warm she felt him all the way down to her toes. Warm and alive and filled with so much power it crackled up her spine, leaving goosebumps in its wake.

She took a deep breath and tried to remember he was the man she was supposed to kill. Otherwise, those idiots in her garden would tell everyone what she'd done. They'd blab about those boys buried beneath the hedges. Those poor boys who had screamed when she took their lives because they'd wanted to do something unspeakable.

Because she'd whispered a spell under her breath and knew they'd done it before.

The memory cooled her heated flesh until she could barely feel his touch any longer.

"It's fine," she replied, stepping away from his hand. "I'll only be here a little while, and I've stayed in worse places."

"Yes, I imagine witches have suffered many odd sleeping arrangements."

She turned around with a spiteful retort on her tongue, only to have the words die. He stared at her with so much heat she was shocked she didn't blister.

The Mountain King licked his lips. A question burned in his gaze. Asking if he delved between the cushion of her mouth, would he find an answer he'd been searching for his entire life?

"Are you twisting my mind again?" she asked, her voice warbling and strange.

"I don't know," he replied. "Why would I want to twist anything when you desire me just as I desire you?"

Morgan had time to slam down the barrier between her

mind and his. This time, she didn't let him cajole her into some foolish stupor. She was a witch! She knew magic and he could not use it against her.

She took a step away from him and shook her head. "No. I came here to kill you, king. And I intend to either do that or go home. Not entertain some tryst in the forest with a faerie who will forget me the moment I leave."

"Who says I will forget you?"

She could see it written in his wild eyes and snarled beard. She could see it in the set of his broad shoulders and how he hadn't even taken the time to put on a shirt. He was a faerie king through and through.

And faeries didn't remember humans.

"I say you will forget," she whispered. "And you can't say that I'm wrong. Because you can't lie."

He frowned, but he didn't reply. Instead, the Mountain King leaned down until his nose brushed her hair. He took a deep breath, inhaling her scent.

Now he had a part of her in him. His magic glowed, hot and strong within her body. And her scent now lived inside his lungs. Magic stirred between them, zinging back and forth in electric sparks.

The king retreated, then bowed. "My lady, you do me the honor of visiting and providing more entertainment than I've had in centuries. My only quarrel is that you think so ill of my kind."

"Faeries are easy to think ill of," she replied. Morgan stepped back into her small "room" and reached for the woven vine door. "Good night, Mountain King. Perhaps you shouldn't sleep too deeply."

"Finding you in my bed at night wouldn't be much of a punishment, witch." A wicked grin spread across his face.

She bared her teeth. "It would be a punishment for me."

He burst into laughter, deep from his belly. "Tell yourself

whatever you must, but there is something between us. Come back to the cottage glen tomorrow. There's a gathering of all the Spring Court. Perhaps you'll change your mind."

"I'll think I'll languish here until Imbolc comes," she replied, then slammed the door in his face.

8

Morgan dreamt of flowers blooming in a field. They were more beautiful than any flower she'd ever seen, but infinitely untouchable. Every time she tried to put a finger against the petals, they withered and died.

Voices whispered in her ear, "Witches can't touch faerie magic. Death will spread wherever you go."

She jolted awake and sat up straight. Sweat slicked her back, sending shivers down her spine and arms.

It wasn't the dream making her cold. She refused to believe that. How was she supposed to sleep in conditions like this? In the frigid air without a ceiling overhead? She wouldn't be surprised if it snowed.

Anger made her cheeks red, but she knew it wasn't the guest room making her upset. Morgan had always used anger as a shield between herself and the world. No one could get underneath her skin if she was a giant bitch.

Rubbing her hands up and down her arms, she tried to ground herself. What could she see? What could she feel? Distractions were the best way to get through the night. The nightmares couldn't hurt her. They weren't real.

Something scrabbled overhead, claws scratching the walls as a creature climbed them. Spiders? Some faerie sent by the king to kill her in her sleep?

Morgan laid back down on her bed of moss and pretended she was asleep. If the king thought to kill her, he'd have to do better than an assassin in the middle of the night.

Witches rarely slept.

She started preparing herself for what she would sacrifice if she needed to kill this creature with magic. Her fingernails were easiest, but they hurt. She could get rid of her hair, magic could cover it until it grew back... But she was vain enough to want to keep her real hair.

Something crawled over the wall and started down the inside. Whatever creature had come to attack her, it crawled toward her with eerie speed and silence.

She held her breath as the moss on either side of her waist indented. It didn't weigh much, likely a faerie the king had sent.

So it was to be like this? If she wouldn't sleep with him, then he'd kill her? Damned faerie.

Something sharp trailed down her forehead and the length of her nose. It paused at the tip, then tapped. "I know you're awake, witch."

Morgan decided on the fingernails. If she needed to attack something, she needed every inch of confidence. She curled one of her hands into fists and felt magic pull out her thumb nail.

She opened her eyes and stared up at the monstrous creature sitting on top of her.

It wasn't a faerie, more a creature of excess magic that had brought sticks and moss to life. The being was made of twigs and a few logs, held together by wayward magic, pulsing between the cracks with green light.

The finger touching her face was made of a few sprigs, though it was missing one appendage and had only a four fingered hand. This creature was little more than magic and earth.

She felt her pointer nail hit the ground and a pulse of magic filled the well in her mind. She could sense the power building, but not enough. Not yet.

This creature was made of the king's magic. Excess power, perhaps. Almost as though he wouldn't know the creature existed.

It tilted its head to the side, and its stone eyes rotated. "You want to hurt me."

"You crawled into my bed in the middle of the night. Yes, I very much intend to hurt you before you attack me."

Before Morgan could pull off more of her fingernails, the creature chuckled. The sound came from deep in its belly. The grinding stones made her ears ache. "I don't intend harm, witch. I want to warn you."

"About what?" She pulled out another nail. Just a few more and she would have more than enough power to knock it back. Then, she could shield the entire room as she should have last night.

She just hadn't thought the Mountain King would be so aggressive.

"The people who sent you here want to keep the king from the throne. They want you to kill him. Don't they?"

How could this creature know about the people who sent her? She'd told no one.

Morgan frowned. "What do you know of the people who sent me here?"

"I know they are dangerous, they are powerful, and you do not know who they really are." The creature of twigs and sticks shifted, now crouched above her with its knees pressed against the moss at her sides. "You cannot kill the king."

"I tried and failed, didn't I? Now I'm stuck here."

Again, the creature laughed. "Stuck or not, you can't kill him."

She pulled out the last nail on her right hand. "If I wanted to kill him, I could. I just need more time to prepare."

"No, witch. I'm asking you not to kill him. He's necessary. He's needed for this world to survive."

She glanced at the walls which shouldn't exist and the trees who were clearly listening to them. They leaned their branches down low, whispering to each other through the leaves. "You don't say? I hadn't guessed he'd made this realm."

The creature spat moss from its stone teeth. "No! He's needed here. We need him to take the throne of power. He won't destroy the world as your strange new bedfellows want you to believe."

Well, it would be useful if she didn't have to worry about killing him. "Why should I believe you over them?" she asked.

"Because I'm from here. I know the king, and they don't."

"I hate to break it to you, but I don't think anyone knows the king." She waved a hand up and down, gesturing to the pieces of the creature. "And you don't look like you've been alive that long."

It wasn't even rotting in certain areas of its wood. She'd seen golems before. Strange creatures animated by magic and sent about to do their master's bidding. They never lasted.

The creature huffed out another breath. This time, a ladybug flew out of its mouth and off toward the moon. "Age is just a number humans make up to convince themselves of power. I am not ancient, but that does not make my knowledge any less."

Morgan felt bad for the creature. It clearly exalted the Mountain King. She supposed she would have as well if his magic had given her life.

The poor thing deserved to speak.

"What do you think your knowledge is then?" she asked.

"What could you possibly say to convince me the king deserves to live? That you are telling the truth while these others are not?"

It shifted closer, excitement glowing in its chest. It stared at her with almost fanatic adoration. "The king is the earth. You are a green witch, you must have felt him."

Oh, she'd felt him all right, and that knowledge terrified her. He was full of magic. So much that she didn't know how to measure it. An ocean in his mind? A body of water so vast, no one could ever plumb its depths?

A being that powerful could obliterate the earth if he wanted. He could use that power to lift mountains higher. To raise the seas and swallow all humans if he wanted.

"I know what you're thinking," the creature said. "If he wanted. That's what you keep thinking in your head. Isn't that the key to all this?"

"What?"

"Killing the king will only transfer the magic to someone else. Another faerie. You will spend the rest of your life hunting the Mountain King through all the hosts." It shifted even closer until the sticks touched her nose again. "Or, you can control the Mountain King in this body. Use the power for your own means."

Morgan was tempted. Following the magic from host to host until all green faeries were dead didn't sound like a lot of fun. "They wanted me to kill this Mountain King."

"Did they?" it asked. "Or did you sign your life away to spend the rest of your days chasing after a ghost? You cannot kill the Mountain King, witch. Only its host. The faerie king is nothing more than a pawn."

If the creature was telling the truth, it sure threw a wrench into her plans. And it wasn't as though the people who had blackmailed her were trustworthy.

She didn't want to kill anyone. Morgan wasn't a black witch

or a blood witch who wanted to destroy the world as they knew it. She didn't thrive off devouring spirits, and she didn't feed her magic with pain.

All Morgan wanted to do was nourish the earth, feel plants grow, and to be left alone.

She made eye contact with the ocean rolled stones the creature had for eyes. "I don't want to kill the king."

It clapped its stick hands. "Good! That's a start. Now, how are you going to control him?"

Morgan shook her head. "I don't want to control him either."

"There is no other choice, witch. You either chase the magic and keep beating it down for all eternity, or you deal with its host."

"I don't want the responsibility of manipulating anyone. He should be able to take care of the magic on his own, or he should die and another host should try. Whatever end he chooses, I want nothing to do with it. I just want to go home."

The creature sighed and leaned back against the nearest tree trunk. The tree was partially the wall, and its bark melded with the creature until it almost disappeared. "You don't get to go home, witch. It was your destiny to come here and deal with the Mountain King. Why deny it?"

"Because I don't want to use anyone," she replied. Vehemence made her words sharp and dagger-like. "Why do you want me to control him, anyway? His magic made you."

"And the magic inside him is so strong. Killing him will solve nothing."

"Neither will turning him into a slave. Isn't that what you're suggesting?"

The creature melted into the tree more, one arm raising and vanishing into a branch. "No, witch. I want you to learn who he is. I want you to listen to him and know the magic. Devour it as you did when you first attacked him. The magic is as much yours as it is his."

With those cryptic words, the creature disappeared into the tree.

"How?" She let out the soft question. It floated in the air like a dust mote and then disappeared.

On hands and knees, she crawled to the tree where the creature had once been. She reached out and pressed a hand against the bark, certain it must still be there and her eyes just couldn't see it anymore.

But all she felt was bark. No twigs, no stones, no magic. Just the ancient song of trees as she'd always felt when she touched the trunk of a well aged oak.

"How is that possible?" she muttered, staring up at the branches twisting overhead.

The tree whispered in the wind. Its leaves told a hushed story of creatures made of magic. Warning signs for changes to come and that she should listen to the creature's words.

"I'm not an oracle," she replied. "The mere idea of the future frightens me. I don't want to listen to a creature built of his magic. How can I trust its words to be true?"

The trees claimed she must be brave. That she should listen.

"I don't even know if I can trust you." Morgan's heart squeezed at the mere thought. Trees had always been her ancient friends. Their roots reached deep into the ground and their stories filled her soul with so much hope. They were the one constant in her life, even after her mother had burned at the stake.

But these weren't just trees. They were trees he'd saved long ago and given a life where they were fed by magic.

Trust us, they sang with dancing leaves and a rain shower of green atop her head. All will be well if you would just learn how to trust again.

Morgan wasn't a trusting woman. She'd been threatened,

beaten, raped, destroyed beyond measure. And that was just in the first fifty years of her life.

Five hundred years more had seen torment at the hands of every single creature that inhabited earth.

"How do I trust anyone?" she asked the trees. "When all I have known is pain?"

9

———

Dappled sunlight through the leaves woke Morgan. She shifted on the moss, tucking her hand underneath her head and blowing out a lengthy breath. For a second, she had convinced herself she was back at her home.

Maybe not in her own bed. The moss didn't feel like her comfortable hammock. But she could convince herself that she'd fallen asleep outside under the stars.

Rolling onto her back, she stared up at the bright sun. The creature from last night... It must have been a figment of her imagination.

Something like that didn't happen. It wasn't some creation of magic who had crawled out of the earth to warn her about the king. No magic was that self aware, even if it was ancient magic jumping from faerie to faerie for generations.

She should listen to the strangers from the garden. They seemed to know what they were doing. And they were blackmailing her. They could ruin her life.

But an innocent man was much more difficult to kill. Especially when he was an innocent man who looked like the

Mountain King. An innocent man with a heart of damn gold because he helped plants and brought them to a place where they would always be safe. For the rest of their long lives.

He even fed them pieces of himself. She couldn't kill a man who was so connected to the earth. And one who'd spared her life.

Morgan grumbled, then rolled to her feet. The sun was high in the sky; its beams burned her eyes.

Her stomach squeezed. She hadn't eaten since yesterday, and even then it had only been breakfast before the visitors had arrived at her cottage. She needed food and water.

The king had invited her to some kind of banquet with his people. Wasn't that what he said? If it wasn't a banquet, then she would force him to give her something to eat.

It made little sense why he was even inviting her anywhere. She'd tried to kill him and showed zero remorse for even trying.

Morgan ducked out of her borrowed nest and backtracked through the forest. This time, the grass didn't help guide her. But she was certain she knew the path. The trees seemed to lean out of her way as she passed.

She placed a hand against the trunk of one and said, "Your king is a rather confusing man."

Leaves showered down upon her head as the tree laughed and agreed. Morgan didn't know many people who would invite a murderer to breakfast. But that's what this faerie king had done.

Shaking her head, she plodded through the forest until she reached the lip leading down into the valley. She stared down in shock, then reached up and rubbed her eyes. Surely her vision was conjuring what she wanted to see.

A giant table had been stretched across the entire glen. A myriad of chairs surrounded it. Each chair was a distinct color, cushion, or made from a unique wood. Even the table had patchworks of different planks across its top.

Nearly every chair was full with varying faeries. Some she'd never seen or heard of before. Flower people, creatures made of trees, a sapling with cherry blossom hair. Her mind couldn't absorb all the faeries seated at the table.

The food atop it was fit for a faerie feast. Breads, honey, and mounds of fruit spilled from the sides onto the ground. She couldn't imagine what had gotten into the king, but apparently he thought their guest deserved a royal feast.

Morgan was painfully aware of her day old clothing, the sweat staining her back, and the leather leggings squeaking with every step.

She supposed it didn't matter. The creatures were waiting for someone, probably her, and she needed to eat.

Her mother's voice screamed in her ears as she descended into the valley toward the table. *Eat no faerie food and drink no faerie wine!*

The legends claimed if a human ate faerie food, they would be stuck in the realms forever. Morgan had always thought that was rather dramatic. Why would she be forced to stay in a place just because she partook in food?

Still, it made her stomach heave a bit. She didn't want to stay here with none of her own people nearby. There was something to be said about being surrounded by the familiar, and not beings made of mud, sticks, and stones.

She reached the table and searched for the Mountain King. He was nowhere in eyesight, but the faeries at the table all wiggled in their seats.

The nearest creature reached out its... arm? She thought? The creature was little more than folded over leaves, like origami, long tendrils of green it waved in the air like wings. Its face was made of delicate folds creating lips, eyes, and brows. "Madame! It's good to meet you."

Not wanting to be rude, she reached out and shook the offered arm. Visions of tearing off its limbs made her palm sweaty as she tried to be gentle. "The pleasure is mine."

The faerie squeaked in pleasure. "Pumpernickel! Did you hear that? A pleasure!"

Another faerie leaned around the first. This one had a head full of petals and blooms splattered down its chest like paint. "It's a pleasure to meet *me*, Cleome. She's probably seen nothing like you before."

Cleome. It was the Latin name for a spider plant. Now that she looked closer, it appeared to be a familiar species.

The creature's face creased in disappointment. "Have you never seen a faerie like me?"

She didn't want to hurt the tiny thing's feelings. "There aren't many of you in the human realm, if any I've ever seen. But it's a pleasure to meet you now. I'm certain the memory will stay with me for the rest of my life."

Cleome straightened with pride. "See?"

The flower faerie snorted. "Sure. We'll see how she does once the king gets here."

Morgan tried to find a seat to take, but there were none. On the rise, she'd thought there were empty spots. Now, she saw those were full of the tiniest faeries she'd ever seen.

Some were little more than dots of pollen. Others were floating waterlilies in bowls of water rested on the seat. So many plant faeries all in the same space. Morgan's palms grew sweaty and her eyes darted from side to side, trying to take in everything she could.

What witch ever got this opportunity? She needed to remember every detail.

The door to the king's cottage slammed open. All the faeries stopped talking and turned as one to greet their king, who strode toward them like a man going to war.

Morgan's tongue thickened and froze in her dry mouth. He was... What the hell?

The king had taken time to clean up. He wore a loose white shirt, open to his belly and revealing the sun tanned planes of his chest. His pants were more modern today. The jeans hugged his thick thighs, and she knew they were molded to the back of him.

His face was chiseled from an artist's dream with brows flicking up at the end, thick and prominent. His nose was long and straight. Vibrant green eyes threatened to burn her to the ground, staring at her with mischief and pleasure.

His hair was brushed into smooth, mahogany locks with a golden sheen from the sun. He'd pulled the mass back into a simple bun at the top of his head, but a few strands fell around his face.

He'd even trimmed his beard. Now he looked less like a wild man and more like a business man who knew an inch of beard could destroy a woman. It was the perfect length to scrape against her face when he kissed her.

Kissed her?

Morgan mentally slapped herself. She was only here until the portals opened, and then she was gone. Never to return.

The king sauntered to her side with a loose hipped walk that made her mouth even more dry. A desert. She had the Sahara desert in her mouth and desperately needed a sip of water.

He stopped less than a foot from her, too close, too big, and far too handsome. He grinned when she didn't say a word. "Cat got your tongue, witch?"

"I don't own a cat."

"Funny, I thought all witches were crazy cat people. Care to explain yourself?"

Morgan knew he was trying to make a joke, but how was

she supposed to be a normal person when he looked like this? Damned fae. They were always so pretty.

Clearing her throat, she looked back at the table instead of him. Perhaps then his beauty wouldn't blind her. "Are the rumors true? Can I not eat or drink anything without being stuck here for the rest of my life?"

A warm chuckle rumbled in his throat. "If we were in the faerie realms, then yes. Faeries used to catch humans all the time for slaves."

Morgan waited for him to explain, but he didn't elaborate. "Then where are we, Mountain King?"

He didn't respond. The damned man was trying to get her to look at him again, wasn't he?

A frustrated huff escaped from between her lips. Morgan gritted her teeth and turned to look at him. "What realm are we in, Mountain King?"

That beautiful face was too much to look at. His gaze was warm, and his smile said he thought she was cute.

She wasn't cute.

She was a five hundred-year-old witch with four dead men in her garden. No one had thought she was cute since the Salem witch trials, and that was just sheer luck.

The Mountain King finally gave in and answered her question. "We're in a realm I made. You can eat and drink whatever you would like here, and nothing will force you to stay."

"Good," she muttered. "Now where am I supposed to sit?"

He turned and gestured behind them. "Beside me, of course. I have given you the place of honor at my table."

That sounded like a trick. Everything here did, however. Morgan hesitated to follow him. If he wanted to make a scene or some kind of ritualistic sacrifice, this would be the perfect time to do it.

"Come, come!" the Mountain King tossed over his shoulder.

"You must be starving after trying to kill me. I know I'm famished after our battle yesterday."

The faeries at the table erupted into chatter. She couldn't catch much of what they were saying, they all talked so fast, but she knew they were distrustful of her.

If only the king had kept his mouth shut, she might have been able to make a few allies. They could have gotten her out of this cursed place without a portal.

Morgan would grind her teeth into nubs if she stayed here much longer. Forcing her jaw to relax was a feat worthy of a champion, but she managed on the lengthy walk to the head of the table.

Two chairs waited for them at the head. One looked like a throne made of an ancient stump. The other was made of saplings, twisted together and covered in pink flowers.

She refused to consider the second chair, the one clearly meant for her, was modeled as a throne. As if he were taunting her.

Morgan sat down, holding onto the arms as though the chair might toss her out of it at any minute.

The Mountain King, on the other hand, sat down with zero qualms. He watched her settle with an amused expression on his face. "No tricks, witch. If that's what is making you sit so gingerly."

"I don't trust a faerie not to have tricks up his sleeve."

He shrugged. "Think what you want. I have no issues with you."

"How is that even possible?" Morgan twisted in her chair to glare at him. "I tried to kill you yesterday. And today you throw a banquet?"

The Mountain King mimicked her movements. Now, they were both turned toward each other like the rest of the table didn't exist.

His closeness was too much. His breath fanned across her

face, smelling of mint and parsley. Earthy and far too tempting for her senses.

She would have moved if his hand didn't snap out like a whip and grab her wrist. "Faeries try to kill each other all the time. You were sent here by a group of people who believe my magic is dangerous. Don't deny it, Morgan, I know where you came from and who sent you."

Her name on his lips hung between them like a drop of water on a leaf. Suspended in beauty and so wonderful, just waiting to fall like a drop of water from a leaf.

Morgan released a small, breathy sound she'd never heard herself make before. "How did you know who they are?"

"I'm a faerie king. I know more than you realize." He squeezed her wrist, then released her. "They're right, you know. You should kill me before the power consumes everything I am."

What?

Before Morgan could force him to explain, the other faeries burst into movement. Dragonfly creatures fluttered into the air and served everyone at the table. Single grapes were tossed onto her plate and she had to catch them before they bounced onto the ground.

A larger faerie, who looked like a tree had pulled itself up by the root, cut a wheel of cheese in the center. A troop of acorns with legs and giant eyes carried a single slice to her plate.

So many faeries bursting into movement and she couldn't speak around the sudden commotion. They were all so loud. So ridiculous.

Their antics reminded her of a circus she'd seen in the early beginnings of America. Contortionists had captivated crowds while dancers had whirled through the throngs and little children had pickpocketed everything they could get their greasy hands on.

But the faeries couldn't take anything from her. She'd brought nothing with her but her magic, and that was all hers.

Except, even this morning she could feel the well in her mind was different. The waters were green now, tinged with algae which had never been in her head before. Her magic had changed now that the Mountain King's power had touched it.

"Eat," the Mountain King said.

The faeries all fluttered back to their seats and tucked into the food with surprising gusto. For creatures who were so small, they could consume a considerable amount of food.

Morgan looked around for utensils. There were none. Faeries apparently didn't use cutlery created by humans.

Sighing, she glanced over at the Mountain King. He ate with his hands, although he made it look graceful. He used the bread as a kind of spoon and barrier between his fingers and the gooey cheese melting on the plate.

"When in Rome, I suppose," she muttered and picked up the bread.

"Rome?" he asked. "I've never been. Is it nice this time of year?"

She popped the bread and cheese into her mouth, talking around the food just to see if such animalistic behavior would annoy him. "Are you trying to make small talk?"

He narrowed his eyes, but didn't comment. "I thought it might make you feel more comfortable to talk about where you came from."

"I'm not Roman."

Her words appeared to surprise him. He blinked a few times, looked down at his food, and then back at her with a sheepish expression. "There are different types of humans?"

Shouldn't he know that? Faeries had helped build Rome. She'd heard stories of their antics in Iceland and seen their meddling in American politics. They were everywhere in the human realm.

She popped a grape into her mouth and asked, "When was the last time you were in the human realm?"

He thought about her question for a long time. "I suppose it would have been 1100?"

"What?" Morgan choked on the grape, coughing hard before she dislodged it. "It's 2020."

"In the human realm?"

"Yes!" Had he not come back to the human realm since then? He'd missed so much. Not just cars and cellphones, but everything. The entire growth of humanity.

No wonder he thought so little of her. He'd only seen humans at their most basic form.

She took a deep breath and another bite of bread. How could she describe her world to him? It would be impossible for someone who had seen none of their developments. "How did you get the clothing you're wearing then?"

"Hm?" He watched a flower faerie who had gotten atop the table and was dancing a jig.

"You're wearing modern clothing."

"Ah, Arcane handles that. Some faeries bring the most marvelous of finds from your world."

The faeries stole things? On the few days the portal was open, she suspected they went hunting. But then why hadn't he been wearing the clothing when she'd first seen him?

Morgan's brows furrowed. He wasn't lying to her about the portals. Faeries couldn't lie. The words would have stuck in his throat and he couldn't have said them at all.

But was he hiding something?

His gaze flicked back to hers. Perhaps he sensed the thoughts going through her head, because his eyes widened in shock a split second before he lunged.

The Mountain King grasped her hands and drew them close to his chest. She gasped, tugged close enough to count the tiny dots of yellow in his eyes. "You could be useful here," he said.

Did he know where her thoughts were heading and knew he had to distract her? Morgan tilted her head to the side and smiled sweetly. "By killing you?"

"No," he said, chuckling with a warm laugh that sent electricity zinging straight between her legs. "You're here until the portals open. You can stay bored out of your mind, or one of my faeries can take you somewhere you can help."

"How do you know I can help?"

"You know green magic, don't you?" The spark in his eyes grew brighter. "You can put that magic to good use here, witch. All you have to do is say yes."

She didn't want to take more of his magic into her. And she wouldn't sacrifice more of herself for these people.

"I guess," she found herself saying. "If I can help, I will."

10

——

Morgan trailed along behind the stone faerie who had collected her from her guest quarters. It had been two days since the banquet and she'd been bored out of her mind.

The Mountain King was right. She needed something to do.

Otherwise, she could only sit in that damned green nest, staring up at the sky. And when her mind was given freedom to wander, all she could think about was him. His broad shoulders. The way his eyes twinkled when he smiled.

The planes of his chest were ridiculous, smooth, and so golden brown she thought they might taste like chocolate. And she loved chocolate.

When was the last time she had lusted over a man like this? She stepped up and over a fallen log. She didn't think she'd ever given a man so much thought or space in her mind.

The king had gotten underneath her icy shell, and she didn't like it one bit.

"Follow!" the rock creature shouted as it rolled away.

The thing had shouted the same order a hundred times since collecting her. She wanted to reply she was not round like a ball and rolling through the forest wasn't possible for a human.

She also knew the faerie wouldn't have any sympathy for her. Its eyes were being mashed against the ground every time it moved. The poor thing didn't know where she was.

"Wait for me!" she shouted back. "I'm not as fast."

"Then walk faster, human!"

They made their way through the trees to another clearing. This one was similar to the valley where the king made his home, but a giant wall of mountains bracketed the back side. Their sheer cliffs seemed impossible to climb.

"What is this place?" she asked.

"The place of doors," the faerie replied. It rolled to a stop in the basin.

She stopped next to it and looked around. This place was barren. Even the grass had died off, almost as though the king's magic didn't stretch this far.

"Why did he want you to bring me here?"

Just as she asked, four portals opened in front of the mountains. Their glimmering green lights were impossible to miss. So beautiful and so promising of her escape.

Morgan held her breath as faeries stepped through with plants in their hands. All the vegetation was dying or nearly dead. The faeries cradled the greenery in their arms like babies.

She should have been looking at the plants. They were the ones who needed her, and she always enjoyed saving a plant when she could. However, her freedom was within reach.

The stone faerie at her feet snorted. "Don't get any ideas, witch. Those are one way portals. If you tried to leave, it would bounce you back twenty feet."

Well, that answered one question. But not the other immediate concern. "The king said no portals could open other than on the solstices?"

The stone faerie's hesitation answered her question. Morgan ground her teeth. The king had twisted his words, just enough to keep her here.

But she wasn't about to open a portal until she knew the complete truth. The last thing Morgan wanted was to be severed in half by magic. She'd seen portals do worse.

The stone faerie rocked back and forth, as if it were gearing up to race away from her side. "The king said you could help the honored ones we bring through the portals. That's your job."

Honored ones? The faeries called plants that?

She watched the stone faerie roll away toward the others who were helping to place the plants in pots. Their drooping leaves and stems were heart breaking. Though the faeries were trying their best, they didn't know how to repot plants the right way.

One faerie with twig arms had thrust a fern up to its neck in dirt and was shoveling loam up and over it. She could hear the poor fern sobbing from here.

Sighing, Morgan rolled up her dirty white sleeves. She'd been in the same clothes for four days now. Might as well get even more dirty.

"Stand aside," she advised. The faeries stumbled back from the pots being carried through the far left portal. "I'll take it from here," she added.

Perhaps they understood her love for plants, or perhaps they didn't want to do the treatments themselves. The faeries rushed away. Each ended up in front of another portal, taking what the next faeries brought through.

So this was what the king meant when he said the faeries brought prizes back with them. They went to the human realm regularly and seemed to bring home trophies along with the plants.

A faerie made of stones stacked atop each other wore a pair

of leggings wrapped around its head. A flower faerie with waterlily petals for hair carried a pair of women's heels along with the drooping ivy in her arms.

Every faerie seemed to come home with something new. Once they deposited their plant with her, they wandered off to huddle in groups. They stared at the items of clothing as though they held the mystery of humanity within them.

Morgan didn't know how to take their actions. Items of clothing were so far from a mystery to her or her own people. It was strange to see anyone ogling over a pair of red heels.

She turned her attention back to the fern. "Come on then darling, let's get you settled."

With a gentle tug, she pulled it out of the loose earth the faerie had shoved it into. She reorganized the loam and put only the roots into the soil.

Now was the hard part. She needed to use magic, or no amount of water and kindness would save the fern. It could barely stand up on its own.

But magic meant she would need to use some of the Mountain King's, and she didn't want to touch the green magic again. It only linked her closer to him. Closer to everything she didn't want to get attached to.

Magic like that was addictive. She could still feel it in her own well, even though she had scrubbed every inch of her mind for days now.

The fern let out a soft whimper that only Morgan could hear. But the pitiful sound was enough to force her to decide.

"Oh, all right," she muttered.

Tugging on the magic deep in the earth was so easy. It shouldn't have been like reaching out for an old friend and asking to borrow a cup of sugar. And yet, it was.

The Mountain King's magic poured through her until her fingers glowed. She reached out and touched a single fingertip to the fern. In an instant, it straightened.

She could hear its sigh. But more than that, she could hear its voice. Like she had the Monstera.

"Thank you," it whispered. The fern's voice was like the tinkling of bells, or ice dripping as the winter melted away. "That's so much better."

"You're very welcome," Morgan replied. What else could she say? She hadn't thought she'd be gardening today, but here she was. Elbow deep in earth and talking to plants.

It felt like home.

She turned to see how many more she had to repot, only to realize there were hundreds of plants behind her. With the Mountain King's magic coursing through her veins, she didn't see them as leaves or stems.

She saw the dead and dying greenery as a war zone. Creatures pulled out of a nightmare and brought to her medical haven. She could save every one, but it would cost her so much. So many sacrifices to be made when she had so little to give.

This was why she hid away in the forest. Morgan couldn't survive seeing the destruction of the world.

She knelt in the dirt with her hands on her knees. Where was she supposed to even start?

A six inch tall faerie waddled toward her with something in its hands. The creature was made of mud and wore a lily pad as a hat. Its eyes were massive though, and bright blue like the crystal clear pond it had come from. "Witch?"

She hated that they called her that. "What is it?"

The mud monster held out a tiny piece of wire. "Explain?" Its voice was far deeper than she would have thought, and raspy.

Morgan took the twisted wire and rotated it in her hands. The brass piece was a cheap bobby pin with a fake pearl glued onto the end. Pretty, but no one would notice it was missing.

She held it up to her head and mimed putting it in her hair. "It holds back hair."

The faerie blinked its large, watery eyes. "Why?"

This one seemed a little more simple than the rest of the faeries she'd met here. Perhaps it was young. Or perhaps creatures in the water didn't talk as much.

Morgan held it out for the mud monster to take. "Our hair gets in our faces sometimes. So we put it back with these."

"Ah." The faerie turned it over in its hands. Its eyes widened when it realized there was a pearl at the other end.

Clearly, her impression of faeries was correct. This one was so enamored with the shiny thing at the end of the bobby pin that it had forgotten Morgan was right in front of it.

She moved to get up and leave the faerie to its shiny object, when it made a frustrated noise.

She paused and glanced back down at the creature. "Yes?"

The mud creature held the bobby pin back out to her with one hand and pointed to her hair with the other. "For you."

Two words this time, a mouthful for something so small. She was shocked the creature would give up something it loved. Faeries weren't giving. She'd never seen one who would gift a treasure, especially one it had just found.

Her heart squeezed in her chest, twisting with an emotion she hated to even name.

Morgan stooped and took the bobby pin. Instead of putting it in her own hair, however, she stuck the bobby pin through the mud right next to the faerie's lily pad. The pearl gleamed in the sunlight.

"There," she said with a soft smile. "Now you look beautiful."

The little creature started giggling. Mud wobbled in every direction as it laughed, then reached up and touched a three fingered hand to the bobby pin. "Oh thank you!"

As it ran away, Morgan crossed her arms over her chest and grinned. Three whole words.

Like a blast of warm air, she felt the king approaching. His magic trailed up her body and tangled around her arms. Like he was the tether to this realm and holding her tight to the land.

She knew where he was long before he stepped closer. Morgan could sense him through the magic pulsing in her chest. The magic made his presence even more powerful.

And even more tempting.

"I see you found your way," he said, coming to a stop behind her.

She stayed facing away, staring at the wall of a mountain instead of the king. "How did you know I was here?"

He shifted, his feet sliding through the sparse grass like the sound of wind in leaves. "I could feel you."

The deep rumble of his voice echoed through her body and mind.

He didn't speak like normal men did. He was not limited by time and space as humans were. It wasn't just his voice she heard, but his power she felt deep in her core.

The bubbling waters of her magic shifted, rolling and reaching for him as though it were alive. She wanted to sink into the waves of his energy and feel them crash over her head.

Morgan tried to breathe normally, in through her nose and out through her mouth. But her lungs insisted she needed to sip the air and taste him on her tongue.

"How?" she whispered, but she already knew the answer.

"You took my magic inside you." He stepped even closer, pausing when his chest heated her back.

Though he didn't touch her in any other way, Morgan felt as though he stroked every part of her body. She wanted to leave the clearing and see what other parts of him she could take inside her.

Because she could still feel him. His magic pulsed and her body reacted without him even having to touch her. He laid not a single hand upon her body and yet...

And yet.

Breathless, she pressed back into him. "Why can I feel your magic so differently than anything else?"

"You've taken magic from a person, haven't you?" He leaned in, and his beard scraped against the soft skin of her neck. "When you share magic with a faerie, there is no deeper connection. You and I are one until you use up all the magic you stole from me."

Dazed, her voice wavered, as it always did when his magic overwhelmed her. "I didn't steal it. You offered me your magic, and I took what was freely given."

Did his lips just touch her neck? She felt as though they did. Something soft and plush had glided over her pulse.

"Freely given?" he murmured. "I don't know if you know the meaning of freedom, witch."

Before she could ask him to clarify, she felt him stiffen and step away. She felt his inhalation like a gust of wind, shoving her toward the stacks of plants and work that needed to be done.

A blast of power shook the ground at her feet. Morgan held her arms out for balance and turned toward the king. "What are you doing?" she snapped before she saw his expression.

His eyes glowed. Not just with heat, but rage. So much rage those eyes looked like chips of emerald, hard and sharp enough to cut through flesh.

The king wasn't looking at her. He was staring at the plants draped on the ground.

Another burst of power shuddered through the ground. A fissure split between her legs and headed toward the portals. Morgan quickly hopped onto one side to avoid being swallowed up by the ground.

A few faeries weren't so lucky. In particular, the mud monster fell into the chasm. It let out a startled shriek and grabbed the edge of the land just in time.

Morgan looked between the faerie and the king, who didn't appear to see what was happening at all. He'd furrowed his brow in anger, his teeth bared, and his eyes glowed with a thousand years of anger behind them.

He had no idea what he was doing, she realized. Not a single bit of control was in that magic.

She dove for the faerie. The mud slipped just before she reached him, but Morgan threw herself over the edge and caught its arm. Hanging by her hips, she blew at the hair in front of her vision and grinned down at the creature. "Got you."

"Witch!" it squeaked.

"Can't let you fall with that pretty bobby pin, can I?" Morgan clawed at the ground and pulled herself up over the edge.

The mud monster was easy to lift. She'd thought it would weigh quite a bit, considering all the mud making it up. It was light, though. Light enough that she could hold it against her shoulder like a baby and carry it far away from the crevice in the ground.

Morgan placed it next to another huddle of faeries and ignored the mud splattered across her top. "There you go," she said. With a quick pat to the top of its head, she turned to the Mountain King.

The man didn't control his magic. She'd seen this happen to a witch before, although it was so long ago she didn't remember how the coven had stopped him. Magic had a way of controlling the user when it wanted.

It was alive inside them. Any magic had a bit of the original bearer's flavor. If that was green magic, it wanted to go back to the earth. If it was black magic, it wanted to be free in the land of the dead.

With the Mountain King, she felt this green magic was older than the rest. It wasn't what she'd dealt with before. This magic didn't come from the earth, nor did it want to go back to the earth.

It wanted something else. Anger had made the ground split open and swallow the back portion of the plants. Rage had popped up the moment he'd caught sight of all the plants laid out.

Morgan approached the king with careful steps. She made certain he could easily hear each movement, and that she remained in front of him at all times. She lifted her hands up to be no threat.

"Mountain King?" she asked. "What are you doing?"

"They destroyed them." The voice wasn't the same as the tempting one she knew. This voice rumbled with the power of an avalanche and the thunder of a landslide. "They know not what they do, and yet they destroy so much."

"Who are they?"

"Your kind, human. All you know how to do is destroy, maim, and kill."

She held her hands up higher, stepping closer. "I'm not human, remember? I'm a witch."

"Even worse. Your kind sacrifices all the things I made. For what? Petty charms and foolish tricks?" His eyes glowed brighter, beacons of verdant green.

Morgan had the distinct impression she wasn't talking to the faerie king at all. This was something much older than the being she knew. Something ancient looking out through his eyes.

"I don't sacrifice green things," she replied. "Don't you remember? You sent me here to fix them. And I did."

"Fixed them?" the creature inside the king snarled. "All I see is dead plants everywhere the eye can fall. How did you fix them?"

Morgan pointed behind her toward the fern still blissfully chirping in its pot, unaware of the surrounding chaos. "I only had time to fix one with your irreverent power. I can fix many more if you let me borrow more of your magic."

The earth stopped rumbling. The fissure stopped splitting open but remained as a scar upon the Mountain King's created world.

Before her eyes, the power dimmed within him. His eyes returned to normal, though wide and panicked.

"What happened?" he asked, his voice shaken.

"I don't think you were here for a bit," she replied. Morgan chose her words, so she didn't startle him even more. "Have you lost control before, Mountain King?"

His eyes widened even further and then, suddenly, he disappeared. Morgan was left to clean up the pieces of distraught faeries and plants who needed saving. And though she wanted to track down the king and yell at him for all he had done, she knew where her place was.

Morgan the witch became Morgan the healer for the afternoon.

11

Morgan wiped the sweat off her brow and looked at the mess she'd somehow cleaned up.

Over a hundred plants were repotted and put into new homes. Some pots were clay, others were plastic. She didn't know where the faeries had gotten them, nor did she care all that much. If they stole, they stole.

She had put some faeries to work. Some were potting plants. They ended the day just as covered in dirt as she was. The others watched stoically and commented when one of the plants needed something.

Morgan had never channeled as much power as she had this afternoon. Every ounce of magic she'd taken from the king was poured into the greenery. The faeries then carted the greenery off to their new homes.

Some pots were bigger than the faeries carrying them, but no one complained. If there was anything she could say about these creatures, they didn't mind hard work.

Yet another recent development she hadn't realized about their kind.

She leaned back on her haunches and nodded at the mud

faerie who hadn't left her side the entire afternoon. "I think we did a splendid job, don't you?"

"Good," it squeaked. The large blue eyes blinked up at her, narrowed, and then focused in on the dirt coating her clothing. "Gross."

"Me?" Morgan placed a muddy hand against her chest. "Gross?"

"Yes."

If the creature had a nose, it would have sniffed the air around her and wrinkled the appendage.

Morgan felt disgusting. Sweat stuck the back of her shirt to her skin, and mud stuck the front to her chest. She'd suffered through a lot of revolting situations in her life, but never had she felt as though she'd taken a bath in a pig pen.

And she'd spent the night in a few pig pens. She never came out looking like this.

She heaved a sigh and nodded. "You know, I think you're right. There wouldn't be a bath nearby, would there?"

The faerie blinked. "Pond?"

She imagined the dirt and mud in a pond, not to mention the little creature's home. She'd turn it filthy in seconds, and then how would the faerie see?

Morgan decided she'd rather know the faerie made it home safe without her ruining its home for a few days. "Is there running water anywhere? Like a stream?"

The faerie thought for a ridiculously long amount of time.

Morgan was about to give up on the idea and tromp back to her dirty nest. Then another passing faerie spoke up. This one had dragonfly wings the length of Morgan's arm on its back. "There's a mountain spring in the caves. I'm sure the king wouldn't mind if you freshened up in there."

"The caves?"

Morgan followed the creature's point to a small hole in the wall of mountains she hadn't noticed. It was barely big enough for the faeries to fit through, but she might squeeze in if she tried.

She shrugged. "All right, then. Anything to be clean, I suppose."

With a pat to the mud faerie's head, she started off toward the cave system. She hadn't been in one for years. The last had been in the 1940s when she found herself on the ocean side of Ireland hunting a troll.

Well, her coven had been hunting the troll. She had been more interested in the creature's treasure trove, rumored to contain a rare, poisonous plant.

Her coven had cursed the troll into a toad. She'd taken the plant while they were all busy.

It was a win-win situation. They didn't want her there, neither did they believe a green witch would be much use. She had healed their wounds before she left, though, and that had given her enough respect to stay within the coven for a couple months more.

Someday, she would leave the coven all together and not feel a bit of guilt for it. They were ungrateful wretches.

Morgan clambered through the small segment of stone. She had to get down on her hands and knees, but could see the caves beyond opened up at least ten feet high. At least she wouldn't be squeezed by the earth.

Standing up straight, she placed her hands on her hips and listened for the sound of water. Maybe she could find a cave system like this back home once she freed herself from the faerie's clutches. Then the coven wouldn't be able to find her. She could still raise plants in here, although none of the ones in her cottage. They needed the sun.

Morgan picked up on a telltale trickling sound and made a sharp right. She clambered down into the abyss, noting spears of light coming from the ceiling. The mountain was hollow, it seemed. And much of the light came from the top where the Mountain King had allowed a few holes to remain.

Did the faeries use this place often? The stones were carved almost into steps, so she could believe this was a place where they bathed.

She hoped there wouldn't be any faeries in here. They were already so fascinated with the human world, she feared what they would do if they saw her without clothing.

Faeries poking and prodding her naked body wasn't on her to-do list today.

Though, she had to admit they were all cute. And she wasn't the person to admit anything was cute. She looked at babies and wondered how anyone took care of one. Human larva frightened her.

Morgan picked her way up and over a stone before descending into an enormous cavern where a stream full of scalding water bubbled. The steam rose in curling tendrils, beckoning her forward for a bath.

Oh god, a real bath.

She unbuttoned her shirt with such speed, buttons flew off in all directions. Who cared? If she had to walk around with her bra only, she would.

The leather pants proved to be more of a problem, however. They stuck to her legs with a suction that rivaled a vacuum. Grunting, she plonked down on a stone and pulled hard enough to release the pants down to her shins.

Toeing off the boots, she pushed everything down onto the floor and left it there. She'd wash the clothing later, but for now, she wanted to get into that water.

Morgan reached behind her for the clasp of her black bra but hesitated at the last second. Maybe she was paranoid. The feeling of eyes on her back were all in her head, not that a certain faerie was lurking in the corner waiting for her to take all her clothes off.

Still, she left on her black underwear.

Wading into the steaming water, she let out a moan that was downright filthy as she sank down to her neck.

Who knew she would miss hot water so much? Actually, she knew. Morgan had gone much of her life without instant baths. She still had nightmares about heating buckets of water over a fire and pouring them into a basin tub.

The water was never hot by the time she got in it. Even magic didn't fulfill the need the way modern day plumbing could.

She let her body float in the gentle moving water for a little while. Centering herself and her magic. All the power was hers and slowly building back up. Eventually, it would be a lake she could dip into again whenever she wanted to.

As she surveyed the waters of her power, she realized it might be a little while longer before she could use her own magic.

She didn't want to give any more of herself to whatever creature she sacrificed to. Whether that was a demon or just the world at large, she didn't want to give more. The magic would build from her own mind if she was patient.

And that was the greatest difference between Morgan and the rest of the witches she knew. They weren't good at waiting, whereas she would wait centuries if that's what it took.

Her magic rewarded her for the patience. Morgan felt more connected to her power than the other witches. She could use it far more to her advantage, and for so much of a smaller cost.

Her soul was hers. And it would remain hers as long as she was patient.

A stone fell from somewhere to her right, tumbling down the stairs and plunking into the water with a harsh slap.

So, she hadn't imagined those eyes after all.

She rolled in the water, placing her feet on the algae covered stones. Crossing her arms over her chest, she sank until the water touched her chin and eyed the only way into the stream.

Had the little mud faerie followed her? She'd have to lecture it on privacy. Or at least letting her know when it were in the same room. No one should be startled while bathing. It was rude.

But the person who stepped down the stairs wasn't the mud faerie. It was the king, once again.

"What are you doing here?" she called out. "I thought you ran off to hide your face in shame."

The words were a little harsh, but she was almost naked in the water. He shouldn't be here. Her stomach twisted into a strange knot at his closeness, and she didn't know if she wanted him in the water with her or so far away she forgot what he looked like.

The king made his way further down the stairs, then stumbled. He righted himself against the wall, but his shambling steps were wrong. Morgan was used to him moving with grace. He might be a sizeable man, but he was always controlled in his movements.

This wasn't the king she had grown used to. This one stomped down the stairs, each heavy step selected with a gaze that didn't look as though he knew where he was.

"Mountain King?" she called out.

He was close enough now for her to see the sweat dripping down his brow. He shook his head like a horse trying to flick a fly away from its face. "Liam," he murmured.

Was that his name? What faerie would ever tell a human, let alone a witch, its name? She could use that against him with just the barest of thoughts.

Morgan opened her mouth to scold him. No sound escaped her lips.

He wasn't feeling well. The droplets of sweat weren't just on his face. They trickled down between the mountains of muscle on his chest. He was sick, or perhaps burning up with magic deep in his core.

Morgan swam close to the edge of the stream into one of the pools, carved from years of running water. "Come here."

His Adam's apple bobbed. Green eyes caught on her form in the water and he shuffled closer. She wasn't certain he had any idea who she was.

The Mountain King knelt by the edge of the water and reached out a hand for her. "Did the king send you?"

"King?"

"The King of Water." He licked his lips, then swallowed.

Was his mouth dry? That was sometimes a sign of poison, although she couldn't imagine who would try to poison the Mountain King.

Liam.

What a lovely name for a man so handsome.

"No," she replied, reaching out with one hand and taking his. "The King of Water did not send me. Do they also call you the King of Earth?"

"All the kings have their names. Each of my counterparts. The four of us took the elementals when no one else would." He licked his lips again. A drop of sweat rolled down his temple and disappeared into his beard.

"Are you feeling well, Liam?" She tried to pull her hand away from his, only to realize he clutched it like a lifeline. She tugged harder, but he still didn't let go of her. "Liam, I need my hand back."

"It's inside me," he muttered. "And sometimes I can't control it."

She stilled. "What's inside you?"

"The magic. The voices. The need to do something about what's going on in the human realm."

Morgan focused her own power, sending it out between them to feel what he felt. The moment she dipped into the green magic pulsing through him, she was slapped back into her own body.

That power was strong. It didn't want her anywhere near the Mountain King's head.

What was the magic planning? It brewed something dark and dangerous deep in the recesses of this faerie's mind. She'd gotten that much before it had slammed the door shut.

"Liam?" she tried again. "You need to get rid of some power. I've seen this before."

"Get rid of the power?" The green magic pulsed through his vision again. The creature or magic or simply the earth looked out at her through his gaze. "I will get rid of no power, witch. Do not try to corrupt me."

"I'm not trying to corrupt you, Liam. I'm trying to help you." He seemed distracted by her body near the portals, so perhaps she could use that to her advantage.

Morgan yanked her hand out of his, aided by the slickness of her skin. She slapped both her hands against the stones and pulled herself out of the pool. Pleasurable things always tempted faeries.

Perhaps it was time to see if she could tempt the king.

Water poured down her body in rivers. It caught in the hollows of her collarbone and the divot of her bellybutton. Her bra was too thin to hide the pebbled peaks of her breasts, but that was the point. She wanted him to look at her. She wanted his attention on her and no one else.

Not even the power that overwhelmed him.

Liam's eyes widened in surprise and then heated with so much lust she wasn't certain she could bear it. He would sear her flesh from bone, just with a single touch.

For the first time in her life, the witch was not afraid of fire.

She reached out a hand, waiting for him to take it. "Liam, you need to use some of that magic."

To his credit, he fought against the boiling in his head. He stepped away from her. The flinching response was almost as though he had seen something. Or predicted what he would do if he touched her.

"No," he muttered. "No I can't."

"Why not?"

"I'll hurt you. If I touch you like this, I don't know what I could do."

She understood that fear. Accidental murder was the worst sort of guilt. "I'm made of magic as well," she replied. "Don't you remember?"

"Your power isn't as great as mine."

"Perhaps not. But I can absorb your magic, Liam. Let me." Although, the mere idea of it made her stomach surge up into her throat. She didn't know how much she could take from him.

All that power inside him could set her on fire. Or perhaps he would use her as a conduit, controlling her like a puppet and fulfilling whatever whim he might have.

Morgan had to help him, though. No other option would suit. So, even without his permission, she pulled.

His head twitched to the side. Moss grew on his shoulders as magic surged in his body again.

It was reaching for her. All that green magic whispering how much it wanted to use her, to live inside her as it lived inside Liam. It desired her just as much as he did.

How strange to be desired by something without a body. But she could hear it in her head. Murmuring, crooning just to let it inside her.

Every inch of her body flushed. Sweat slicked her skin, not from some sickness. She wanted him. She wanted whatever lived inside him with so much need that her knees felt week.

"What is it that makes me desire you so?" she asked. "Is it just because you're a faerie king? Is this what it's like to be in the presence of all fae royalty?"

Liam shook his head and groaned, "No. No, it's never like this."

At least she wasn't crazy. He felt it too.

Another ripple of power passed through them. A wave of pleasure so strong rolled over her body that her toes curled. Morgan tossed her head back in ecstasy. She'd never felt this before.

Her entire body clenched. Deep between her legs, a pulse started like a heartbeat. The feeling burrowed deep into her soul. She could feel him in her head, in her magic, in her body.

Mouth open, she tried to control herself but couldn't. Everything was wrong and right and so infinitely powerful.

"Liam," she whispered, breathing shallowly. "What are you doing to me?"

She dropped her gaze to see he'd grown horns made of tree limbs. Moss grew on his shoulders and trailed down his chest. Flowers bloomed in his beard and leaves unfurled on the branch horns.

He wasn't just a faerie, anymore. He was something more. A god made of earth and spring. He was life itself, bringing a new age with him she couldn't even have dreamt.

He reached for her and smoothed his thumb over the peak of her cheekbone. "Morgan."

"What are you doing?" she repeated, still trying to catch her breath.

"I don't know."

Liam tugged her closer until she could breathe in his exhalations. Pollen floated out of his lips. She inhaled every bit, bringing his magic deep into her lungs and even more into her body.

His sturdy arms curled around her back. He held her so tenderly and yet, she knew she couldn't get out if she struggled.

Her thighs quaked as another wave pulsed through her. His heart beat against hers, ragged and thunderous. His sweat slicked her skin. She could feel every inch of him against her, warm and wet and wonderful.

"I shouldn't do this," he muttered. His lips were close enough so she could feel their heat. "You deserve better than this."

"I said I wanted to help, didn't I?" Morgan didn't know what she was saying. She feared everything she would do if he continued. He would turn her into a puddle of woman at his feet and she would beg for more.

The magic in his gaze dimmed until it was just Liam, the faerie king she recognized. Clearing his throat, he released her and repeated, "You deserve better than this."

He melted out of her arms. Leaving only the lingering scent of peat and loam to comfort her.

12

───────

Morgan gathered her things and left the hot springs with a pressing question on her mind. He'd grown branch horns and moss on his shoulders... What was he?

The tinge of his green magic inside her flashed with a vision. Not horns, but a crown. And not just moss, but a mantle of earth that rose from the ground and trailed behind him, spreading green things in his wake.

But it wasn't just green. The harder she looked into the vision, the more she saw faces frozen in the moss and flowers behind him. Human faces, frozen in horror with mushroom caps growing atop their heads.

He wasn't just going to be a king. He would be the end of the world as they knew it.

She crawled out of the caves with her clothes in her hands, not caring that she was in nothing more than her underwear. She'd wash the clothes later when she had the time. For now, her mind was running a mile a minute.

The Mountain King was controlled by powers she couldn't fathom. That magic was old. Ancient even, but older than any she'd ever come across before. And she'd dealt with thousand year old vampires and gnomes born from lava fields. None of them held a candle to the magic she had touched today.

Morgan wasn't looking where she was going. Her feet carried her somewhere, but she didn't know where.

A sharp pain struck her ankle, bringing her down onto one knee.

With a hiss, she slapped her palm against the sudden ache. Her fingers touched a smooth, scaled back slithering away.

With a snarl, she glared at the garden snake sitting in the tall grass. "Arcane."

"Well I wasn't getting your attention any other way, now was I? Someone is distracted." He flicked his tongue, and she had the distinct impression he wanted to bite her again. "Humans never look where they're going."

"You would be distracted too if the Mountain King had turned into a world ending god in front of you," she muttered, still rubbing her ankle. Twin beads of blood bloomed every time she released her hold, and Morgan didn't want to leave any trace here.

Blood was the ultimate way to control someone. Even more than a name. She might be foolish, but she wasn't careless.

Arcane stiffened. He arched his back until he stood on the very tip of his tail. He stared into her eyes with his slitted yellow ones, and whispered, "What did you just say?"

"You know what I said. Your king is terrifying when he wants to be."

Arcane flicked his tongue again, tasting the air. Scenting for a lie? "Yes, he is."

"And I have a feeling all that power isn't Liam, is it?"

The snake sank back to the ground and slithered back and forth. Pacing, it seemed, in the only way a snake could pace. "He told you his name?"

"I don't think he meant to. He wasn't himself."

"No, that power doesn't make him the faerie we all know." Arcane twisted his body around a small stone, then started his circling again. "Where were you?"

"The hot springs."

"Who told you about those?" He paused and looked up at her with wide eyes. "You aren't supposed to be in there. Those are the king's private bathing chambers."

"The faeries." Had they tricked her? Were they trying to play some strange version of faerie matchmaker she wasn't privy to?

Arcane huffed out a lengthy breath. "Damned things. They know they shouldn't be in there, and yet they still sneak in whenever the king isn't looking. As if he doesn't know when someone disturbs the waters."

Faerie matchmaker indeed. Morgan's cheeks burned with embarrassment, even though the snake didn't know what she'd been thinking. Matchmaker! The faeries shouldn't want their king to end up with a human, let alone a witch.

They might like her, but she wasn't queen material. She knew that more than anyone. Shaking herself free from such thoughts, she stood. "Well, I'm going back to my nest, then."

"No you aren't." Arcane stretched his body up, reaching his head toward her. "Pick me up."

"What?"

"Up, woman."

She couldn't imagine this would be pleasant for either of them. Being carried was rather degrading, and she didn't want to hold the snake who hated her. He'd already bitten her once.

Still, he seemed to know what he was doing. So she sighed, leaned down, and lifted him.

Arcane eased his way up her arm and wrapped around her bicep. He tightened until it felt as though she were wearing some piece of jewelry, not a living creature. "To the cottage," he said.

"Why would I go to where the king is?"

"Trust me, the king isn't in the cottage. If he's losing control again, then he'll be going somewhere he can be alone."

"Why?"

Arcane tightened to the point of pain. "Don't ask questions, human. Just do what I tell you."

She wasn't great at taking orders, especially from someone who disliked her. But in this case, she supposed she didn't have a choice.

Morgan strode out of the gully and back up into the forest beyond. As she passed under tree branches and clambered over logs, she tried to remain silent. Arcane wasn't chatty either until they were very close to the cottage.

"Why are you in your underthings?" he muttered.

"I was taking a bath."

"You're still carrying your clothing. You could put them on."

She waved them in the air so they both were blasted with the scent of stale sweat, mud, and body odor. "I don't think I want to put them back on until they're clean."

He coughed. "Why didn't you wash them in the hot springs then? Petunias and hyacinth, that's a horrible smell! Is that what humans always smell like?"

"No," she replied with a chuckle. "That's what humans smell like when you don't let them bathe regularly."

"Yet another reason I'm glad to be the familiar of a faerie and not a witch." Arcane breathed through his mouth for the rest of the journey.

She would have preferred any other faerie to travel with. But he was rather humorous, she supposed. Certain parts of his antics made her chuckle, so maybe that's why the Mountain King kept him around.

Liam, she corrected. Every time she thought of him as the Mountain King, something inside her whispered more. She knew his name now. And it was a beautiful name that sighed in her head like wind through leaves.

Maybe that was his magic.

Morgan drew the shields of her own power a little tighter. Just in case. Liam didn't appear to be in his right mind and someone who was out of control could poke around within the headspace of another.

She would be careful. Just in case.

Up and over the rise, she carried Arcane and down into the valley with the small cottage beyond. The door was back on its hinges, as she'd noted at the dinner. Everything had been cleaned from their banquet as well. No more table, chairs, or even a speck of food on the ground.

She strode into the middle of the valley, then paused. "Well? What are we doing here?"

"Getting you some proper clothing, apparently," he muttered. Arcane released his hold on her bicep and slithered down to her hand. "Put me down, I'll take you there."

"Where is there?" she asked as she set him on the ground.

"It's not some kind of magical place, witch. Not everything is an illusion in faerie realms." He grumbled all the way to the front door where he reared up and poked the wood hard with his face. "Open it."

She reached forward and hesitated before she touched the wood. Was he in there? She didn't know if she could survive another round of energy like that.

Morgan had purposefully not thought of the orgasm worthy waves, how they had made her body feel so… strange. It wasn't like physical pleasure, instead it was mental pleasure that made her feel like a goddess.

If he was capable of that without even trying, what would he do if she gave in to him? She wouldn't be the same woman after a night in his bed.

Maybe the stories were true. All witches knew of human

women who returned as blithering idiots after spending too long in the faerie realm. The faerie-touched would only speak of the man who had stolen their hearts.

Morgan could understand their addiction if she'd experienced only a fraction of what human women felt after a night with a faerie.

Arcane tapped the door with his face again. "Witch. Door. Now."

She ghosted her fingers over the smooth, sanded wood. "This threw me back ten feet the last time I tried this."

The snake sighed and put his forehead against the entrance. He stared at the ground for a few minutes before he finally responded. "The king isn't in there. You're welcome in his home now since we know who you are. Just open the damned door. I'm trying to be nice for once."

Well, if he was trying, then she supposed she should try as well.

Morgan opened the door and let the snake into his master's domain. She stepped into the cool room and goosebumps spread across her body like the pox. Shivering, she stared at all the changes.

It was as though they'd never fought. Every floorboard was where it should be. All the pots were in one piece again and the plants were happy.

She could hear them in her head. Some were singing little ditties about sunlight and growing. Others were whispering about the witch who had returned. One was silent, but if she listened to the spider plant hard enough, she could hear it snoring.

For all intents and purposes, it appeared nothing had happened here. How was that possible? She'd seen the faeries carrying the pots into the realm. And then she'd used all those new pots.

Had he used magic to put everything back together? She

didn't think that was possible for faeries like him. Green magic affected only growing things.

Although, he had created an entire realm with that power. And building realms had little to do with plants or helping them grow. So maybe Morgan didn't know as much about his magic as she thought.

Arcane slithered toward a door in the back, beside the one leading to Monstera. She could feel the plant on the other side of the cottage and sensed its roots growing deep through the floorboards.

"Come get something on, witch," Arcane spat. "There's a chest in the back corner of this room. Should have something that will fit you."

Morgan set her clothing down on a nearby table and then made her way to the door. Opening it revealed a bedroom beyond. Not much of one. Just a chest of drawers on the left, a plain oak bed, and then a small table with a lamp. The chest was at the foot of the bed. Everything else looked as though it hadn't been touched in years.

Was this his bedroom? She stepped into it, holding her arms over her chest even though no one was in the room to see her.

Yet, somehow, it still felt as though eyes were on her.

The chest lid creaked as she eased it open. Everything inside smelled of mildew and moth balls, but the dress on top was beautiful. She'd never been much of a dress person, even back in the days when women were required to wear them.

But this one... it was beautiful.

White silk spilled down from the shoulders, creating a deep V in both the front and the back. The style was almost Grecian, and she had a feeling it might be that old.

Gently, she pulled it out of the chest and let the fabric ease onto the floor. The silk was so fine it felt like spiderwebs in her hands. Spilling out of her arms and pooling at her feet, this was far too fine a dress for her to wear.

She turned back to Arcane, shaking her head. "I can't wear this. I'll ruin it. Dirt on something like this would be…"

Her words failed her. It wasn't Arcane in the entrance. It was Liam.

Moss still covered his shoulders, though the branch crown had disappeared. He braced himself on the doorframe with both arms, leaning into the room. His biceps bulged as though he were holding himself back. Even the veins in his arms stood out prominently.

He wasn't staring at her with anger, as she feared. Instead, the heat in his gaze seared her to the core.

Morgan took a deep breath. "Arcane brought me here."

"I know."

She held the dress in front of her like a shield. "He said I could wear something from the chest, but this is far too fine."

His throat worked in a heavy swallow. "No. It's perfect."

"I'll get it dirty," she tried to argue. She didn't want to be beautiful in front of him. She wanted to just be the woodland witch with crazy hair and dirty skin. Someone unremarkable and forgettable.

When people remembered witches, they started fires. A faerie king remembering her? She couldn't bear to think centuries would pass before she didn't have to look over her shoulder for him anymore.

Liam released his hold on the door and strode into the room. Petals fell from the flowers still tangled in his hair, leaves dripping from him like rain.

He took the dress without a word. Silent, he scooped his arms through the bottom then held it over her head. Waiting.

She couldn't suck in enough air to satisfy her lungs. The Mountain King, the Earth King, a faerie king was dressing her? He stood so patiently, waiting for her to lift her arms so he could slide the most beautiful white dress she'd ever seen in her life over her head.

Heart thundering in her chest, she lifted her arms.

Liam guided the dress down. He slid his hands over her forearms and biceps, leaving behind sparks of electricity like he'd planted them beneath her skin. Heat prickled wherever he touched.

She lost her breath when he touched her ribs. His palms were just an inch away from her breasts, and he must feel her thundering heartbeat. He must feel the heat of her body and knew she was waiting for something, anything.

Warm hands glided down her ribs and the sides of her stomach. Everywhere he touched was on fire. Then the silk cooled her with icy fabric.

Liam met her gaze, and she saw so much passion in his eyes. He was still in control, but barely. She could see the glowing embers of desire and they reflected a need that made her heart race and her lungs ache.

Slowly, he knelt before her. Easing down onto his knees so he could glide his hands down her hips, thighs, and calves.

She looked away from him. A faerie king kneeling at her feet was too much. Far too much for a mortal woman.

"Morgan," he rumbled.

Her cheeks burned, a blush spreading from her face to her chest. He'd dressed her. Why had he dressed her when all she wanted was for him to take the dress off?

She had to resist him. He was a faerie, and she already knew he would ruin her.

She liked her life alone. Every inch of her home reflected Morgan, and every inch of herself was who she wanted to be. No one else affected her life. She couldn't let a man wander into her soul and reset everything she'd accomplished.

Liam stood. His beautiful face was all she could see. The

high planes of his cheeks, the elegant long nose, the close-cropped beard that felt so good against her neck.

"You said I deserved better," she whispered, a last ditch effort to push him away even though she didn't want him to go.

He lifted a hand and cupped her face. His fingers curled along her jaw and tunneled into her hair at the back of her head. "I was wrong."

Liam tugged her hard against him. He devoured her with a kiss that seared her to the bone. She could taste honeysuckle on his tongue, a burst of flavor like she'd bitten into a mango, and something earthy like the bitterness of kale. He tasted of all the green things in the ground while pouring magic into her as though she were a vessel to contain him.

He clutched her waist, his fingers almost bruising. Liam held her as though she were the fields upon which he toiled. As though he could sow flowers and life into her body.

So he drank in the air from her lungs. He conjured her soul to the surface of her skin until she could feel him there as well.

He consumed every piece of her body, mind, and spirit.

Seeds she didn't want grew in her heart and in the deep well of her magic. Seeds that bloomed into petals so glorious, so glimmering, she knew she'd never be the same again.

His tongue swept between her lips, and she shuddered. He reached up and palmed her breast, massaging until she stopped being and only felt. His thumb pressed hard against her nipple, then soothed with a gentle flick.

He knew how to play her body like a musical instrument and she didn't even know where she was.

The fleeting thought terrified her.

Morgan had never lost control like this. Not once in her life. Magic could only run rampant when the owner was unaware. Thus, she was always in control.

Always.

Planting her hands hard on his chest, she pushed away

from him. He let her go without complaint, but it still felt wrong.

She wanted nothing more than to be in the heat of his arms again. Just a second out of them, and she desired him even more.

How was that possible?

Shaking her head, she darted around him and toward the door. "I'm sorry. That should never have happened. I shouldn't have let that happen."

He stood with his back to her, stiff and straight as a tree trunk. He didn't respond.

Morgan wouldn't apologize, she couldn't, not when her thoughts were running through her head. She fled the room, the cottage, and valley where she felt a part of her soul detach from her being and drift back into his arms.

13

———

Morgan slapped at the branches slowing her retreat. She didn't want to go back to that place with the soft moss and a ceiling made of stars. He'd created it for her. Which meant he could come there any time he pleased.

There wasn't even a lock on the door. Morgan couldn't create one from magic, because all her spells were partially his now. Green magic glowed in her well of power, familiar energy yet not her own.

What had they been thinking?

What had *she* been thinking?

He was a faerie king. He was dangerous, far more than just a normal faerie with its pretty eyes and cajoling grin. She'd met faeries before and not a single one had tempted her.

This one shouldn't differ from all the others, she told herself. Maybe he had more power, and he was more interesting with his story and abilities. And she'd never met a faerie who cared about the earth the way Liam did.

His green magic called to her, that was all. Not the beautiful grin on his face when he'd sank down onto his knees before her. Not the heat in his palms that spread through her skin like sinking into a warm bath. And it wasn't the honeyed taste still coating her tongue.

She scrubbed the back of her hand over her lips. She needed to get him off her. His taste, scent, touch. All of it had to go, or she would lose her mind.

The trees tried to reassure her. They whispered there were worse things than kissing a faerie king, and it didn't matter how his touch had branded her. He was an honorable man to the core, and she could do much worse.

"I don't want to do worse or better," she snarled. "I didn't want anyone in my life. I was perfectly happy on my own before being blackmailed into coming here. Don't you see? I don't need him."

An oak beside her sighed. Leaves rained down on her as it shook its branches. "No one needs anyone, little witch. Sometimes they fall into our lives to help just because they can. Not because you need them."

Well, she didn't like that answer either. Morgan slapped another branch. "It doesn't change my feelings, oak. Now get out of my way."

They let her pass, although she could hear their mutterings the entire way. They weren't happy with her choice to run, and frankly, neither was she.

Her entire body ached with need. She was angry, frustrated, and even worse, she didn't like herself right now. Morgan wanted to run back to the cottage and throw herself into his bed.

How bad could it be?

The well of magic deep in her body throbbed with an old pain. A pain she remembered all too well.

Draining her magic for another person would only lead to worse heartbreak than now. She'd give him every piece of herself, and he would take and take and take. Wasn't that what people did?

They used others until there was nothing left for the person to give. Then, they moved onto the next useful person who might give them something more.

Faeries were takers, just like humans. People like them knew how to get what they wanted. And once they weren't getting what they wanted anymore, then it was onto the next best thing.

He was a faerie king! He could have any woman he wanted. Right now, he wanted her. While that was all well and good for a distraction, she didn't need a distraction. She had to get out of this realm. Back to her plants, and her lonely little cabin in the middle of the woods.

Morgan paused and braced herself against the trunk of a tree. Lonely. It was the first time she'd ever thought of herself as lonely.

What was he doing to her?

Now her own life wasn't as satisfactory because of one damn kiss?

This wasn't like her. And she didn't appreciate the massive shifts in who she was as a person. This was just a man. Just a few months and a drop in a very large pond of her life. She could survive through this without losing more of herself.

The bark of the nearest tree warped, revealing a strange face with glowing green magic deep inside it. Stone eyes rolled from the back of its head to meet her startled gaze.

The creature from the middle of the night? What was it doing here?

She had somehow convinced herself their meeting was a conjuration of her mind. She wanted to think something here planned to keep the king alive. That was all.

But here the creature was. In the flesh.

Twigs became its mouth, stretching from the tree into

warped lips. "I told you to get close to him, not to lose your heart."

Morgan snarled. The sound came from deep within her belly where the animalistic witch inside her lived. "I don't care what you told me to do. I'm not doing anything here because you ordered me to do so."

"Well you should listen to me."

"Why?" she asked.

Morgan stumbled back as the creature peeled itself from within the tree. She tripped, tumbling over a fallen log behind her and landing hard on a bed of moss.

The creature appeared taller this time. The branches of its legs were thicker, more stable as it lumbered forward.

Thankfully, it didn't straddle her as it had last time. Instead, the creature sat down upon the log she'd tripped over. Its knees were made of rocks, she realized. In fact, every joint was a rock allowing the sticks of its body to swing.

The creature leaned its earthen forearms on its legs and watched her with a blank, stony gaze. "You've seen what he could become."

She gulped. "I'm no oracle," she said, although the words felt wrong.

"You keep saying that," the creature replied, "but maybe you have a little oracle in you after all."

"No. The coven of witches tested me. They said the only magic in me was green, and weak at that."

"Hm." The creature reached up and plucked one eye out of the socket. Once released from the socket, the eye glowed with the power that gave the creature life.

It held its eye out for her to take. She told herself it was just a stone. She'd picked up a hundred stones in her life and none had made her feel nauseous to hold.

But this was an eyeball. It had been in the creature's head, looking at her. Morgan swallowed her disgust and reached for the rock. She held it in her palm only for it to roll over and look at her.

The creature hummed. "There's more magic in you than the first time we met."

"I helped heal some plants the faeries brought back from other realms," she replied. "I had to take some of his magic to help."

"That's good. The more magic you take from him, the less he can use." The eye rolled again, this time staring between her breasts and beyond. She could feel the creature's old magic reaching into her heart and surveying the magic of her soul. "It's changed your power, you know."

"No," Morgan denied the implication. "My magic is still my own. I've kept the two separate because I know the danger."

"Not very well," the creature replied. "I can see him in you. And if I follow the connection, I can see you in him."

Morgan felt her heart stutter and then slow. Her in him? How was that possible?

She couldn't imagine he'd taken any of her magic. She would have felt the ripping of energy from herself. No one had ever taken something she hadn't given, not without her knowledge.

But he was a faerie king. He could do a lot of things others couldn't.

Shaking her head, she crab walked away from the creature. "No, no, all my magic is right where it's supposed to be."

"Don't run from me, Morgan."

"I don't want to talk anymore. I don't even know who or what you are."

"Morgan, stop moving." The words rang with the power of her name. Faeries chains surrounded her ankles and wrists, forcing her to stop. Pinning her to the ground.

This was why she didn't want any faeries knowing her

name. This was what she had feared the moment her name was uttered in this realm.

The tree being stood, its knees creaking. Every step toward her shook the ground, and she would swear the creature got larger as it moved closer. As if the forest itself was feeding it with more sticks, stones, and moss.

It knelt before her in a mocking bow. "I am the embodiment of this forest. The trees gave birth to me when they were first brought here, as their mouthpiece and their caretaker."

She forced her mouth to open. "The king never mentioned you."

"The king doesn't know I exist." It placed a hand on the ground and lady's slipper flowers bloomed where it touched. "He only knows something in this forest protects him when he needs it. And now, he needs protection more than ever."

"I'm just one woman," she whispered. "I don't know how to protect a king, nor do I think I'm the right person to do so. I was hired to kill him and failed! He can protect himself."

"I'm telling you to protect him, witch. And if I'm telling you, then that means the trees are. The land that cradles you requires your help." The eye in her hand rolled out of her grasp and back to the creature. It picked up the stone and popped it back into the socket. "You don't have a choice in the matter."

14

———

Morgan couldn't sleep. She stared up at the moon above her nest and wondered why she felt so... strange.

After her conversation with the forest being, she couldn't get its words out of her head. The Mountain King was inside her? She'd spent hours in the sequestered pools of her own powers, kept separate from his borrowed magic, but she couldn't find a hint of green.

It was all her magic. All the way it should be.

Sure, there was more magic than she'd thought there would be so soon after depleting it. That wasn't all so surprising while she was in the faerie realm. She knew time passed slower here than in her world.

But then again, Liam had claimed this wasn't the faerie realm. Maybe time passed the same as it did in the human realm.

She didn't know what to believe. Was her magic growing faster because some of his had melded with hers and she couldn't see it?

She should have been disgusted that a faerie had somehow

left his mark inside her. Any self-respecting witch would have funneled all her magic into the ground and made sure there wasn't the tiniest bit of faerie inside her. Her coven would have destroyed every bit of her magic. They would have tried to exorcise the creature from her skin, soul, and mind.

The responsible thing would have been to do exactly that. Scrub her mind clean of him, and any lingering faerie influence.

But she couldn't let him go.

Her mind wondered what the world would look like without the green magic. The veins of emerald still hovered at the edge of her vision. She could see where every single plant was tied to this realm and all the glimmering power.

The world was more beautiful because she could see all this. It was lovely and wonderful and so different from the human realm. Giving that up felt like giving up her ability to see color.

It wasn't necessary for her to see the magical ties, but it made the world a better place.

She sat up in her nest and scrubbed her hands over her face. Sleep wouldn't be coming tonight, apparently. All she could manage was arguments with herself.

"Get ahold of yourself, Morgan," she grumped. Her mind wouldn't listen.

If she wasn't thinking of her magic, then she was thinking of that kiss. The kiss that had branded her for the rest of her life.

How was any other man going to live up to that?

Such a stupid thought. Men didn't have to live up to each other and comparing anyone's kiss to another was foolish. She was only hurting herself with thoughts like these.

Groaning, she sat cross legged in the middle of the nest and held her head in her hands. Tunneling her fingers through her tangled locks seemed to help. She could tug a bit and the pain put her back in the place where she needed to be. She had to remember this was only temporary, and she had survived worse than handsome faerie men who consumed her thoughts.

"You're fine," she whispered. "There's no one else here but you. You can control whatever you have to control."

Breathing deeply, she centered herself.

Except, when she opened her eyes, she realized centering had only made things worse. Tiny stones floated in the air. No, not stones. Crystals had been pulled out of the earth, their holes still open in the ground where her power tugged.

The moonlight glimmered on their sharp edges. All different crystals, each beautiful and wondrous, but so horrifying.

She wasn't in control.

Each crystal was a distinct type to help with anxiety. She reached for one, plucking it from the air where it floated. The amethyst was nearly perfect. The pillar would have made a fantastic wand back when witches still used them.

Morgan allowed the smallest bit of her stress to flow into the stone. And to her horror, it glowed green.

The creature had been right. Liam's magic lived inside her own. She couldn't control it any more than he could.

Morgan dropped the crystal into her lap and blew out a long, low breath. She was so screwed.

Suddenly, the nest felt like a prison. She was trapped in these walls he'd made, and everything was changing. Even her own magic no longer felt familiar or welcoming. Morgan wasn't herself. And a witch who wasn't herself was more dangerous than an atomic bomb.

Scrambling from her mossy bed, she tossed herself out of the nest and into the forest. Moonlight followed her. Tendrils of light grabbed at her shoulders, trying to hold her in the safety of her borrowed room. But it was all too much.

Anxiety pressed at the back of her throat. She would vomit if she stayed trapped any longer.

Tumbling out onto the forest floor, she realized even that didn't release the tension. The forest wasn't a haven for *her*. It was just as much a prison as the rest of this realm.

He was in every bit of the construction. She saw his broad shoulders in the strength of the trees. His smile in the delicate veins of the leaves. His laughter in the moss trailing up the tree trunks.

Liam was the mastermind of this place. If she loved the land, then she must feel the same way for the constructor.

But she didn't. Couldn't. Even feeling *fondness* for a faerie was a death sentence. He'd take her heart and stomp on it. He'd twist it up into a poisonous ball and force feed it to her the moment she tried to leave this place.

Faeries weren't kind.

They didn't bring back plants from the human realm just to put them into pots and heal them. They didn't whisper sweet nothings in her ear and stop themselves from taking what they desired. And they didn't hold themselves bound to a code of honor that allowed a woman to leave their room without paying a debt.

Breath catching in her lungs, she struck the tears from her eyes and stumbled through the wood. Away from the nest. Away from the trees.

She couldn't stand to be here anymore with so many eyes on her. The trees judged her actions. They whispered questions, asking why she couldn't just let go.

"I've been trying my entire life," she whispered through tears. "I can't do it."

All her life she'd been searching for something. Someone. Maybe it was just the idea of someone who could ease her out of this horrible place in her life where she was stuck. Alone.

But she didn't want anyone to change the way she did

things. Morgan liked her life the way it was. Adding people to her plan made maintaining her routine difficult. She remembered the first man she'd fallen in love with. How wonderful his kisses had been and how his arms had turned into a safety net from the world.

Until he found out she was a witch. He'd been convinced she would sacrifice him to the devil and ran from her so fast he'd tripped and fallen onto a rake.

Morgan had made him promise to tell no one what she was. If he'd ever loved her at all, he had to keep her secret or he would bear the burden of her death.

He'd agreed. But he'd worn the scar from the rake for the rest of his life. Others had asked what happened between them, and he always said the same thing. "She wasn't who I thought she was."

The next man had thought she was too wild.

The next that she was too tame.

The most recent that she hadn't applied herself in witchcraft enough, and her quaint life was a waste.

Every single person wanted something different from her until Morgan didn't know who she was.

She burst out of the trees and down into the gully where the portals were. Her lungs heaved in air as though that could dispel her panic. Her muscles ached with tension she couldn't release no matter how hard she tried. All the ghosts of lovers past whispered in her ears.

Not good enough.

Not pretty enough.

Not a talented enough witch.

She had spent her life being less than what someone had expected and now people wondered why she was so closed off? They claimed she was too cold for anyone to love. So many people wondered why she was callous, rude, why she pushed people away. She was the creation of their disregard and disdain.

She fell onto her knees where the portals had opened. Her breath sawed in and out of her lungs. A panic attack swelled through her body. Burying her deep in regrets until she couldn't breathe through the grave dirt filling her lungs.

Morgan let her head fall back and her mouth fall open, sawing in a breath. She stared up at the moon that looked so similar to the one she knew and loved. The moon that had given her the gift of femininity and forgave her for so many failings.

"Mother moon," she whispered through thick tears. "I just want to go home. Please, won't you help me go home?"

Wings fluttered in her ear. Dragonfly wings that scraped against each other like glass. "Witch? You want to go home?"

All Morgan wanted was a few moments to have a breakdown in private. She didn't want to talk to another faerie who would try to convince her to stay. Or worse, report back to their lord and king what had happened.

Her shoulders slumped forward, and she pressed her hand against the soil. "Yes, I want to go home."

The faerie fluttered into view. She was no larger than Morgan's pointer finger. A flower petal dress covered her very human body, and dragonfly wings moved so quickly behind her they were little more than a silver blur. Her hair was bright green. Everything here was unique, at least she could appreciate those details.

The faerie hovered just before Morgan's gaze. "Why would you want to go anywhere?"

How could she explain anything to a creature who loved this realm? She didn't want to confuse the faerie. Or worse, taint its experience.

But she couldn't lie to it either. They deserved to know why she felt stuck. "I can't be alone here. Ever."

"No one is ever alone," the faerie replied. A soft grin crossed her face. "The earth is always with us. The air is always giving us life, and the water is always lulling us to sleep. Fire always keeps us warm. The four kings keep the entire world alive."

The four kings. The ones who were supposed to take their thrones and then end the world.

Faeries wouldn't care. They'd be fine after their leaders took control. Humans would be the ones to leave, suddenly and in horrible ways.

She remembered the vision of human faces stuck in moss. Mushrooms... there had to be a clue in that. Or perhaps it was merely the horrible truth. The world would end whether or not she succeeded in placating the Mountain King.

Morgan tried a smile, though it felt brittle on her face. "It's not the same. In the human world, I'm alone all the time."

"It sounds lonely."

There was the word again. *Lonely.* Like the mere thought was a curse everyone should try to avoid.

"No, it wasn't lonely," she corrected. "It was *lovely* to be on my own and live the way I wanted to."

Even if sometimes she stacked pillows at her back so she could feel like someone was in bed with her. Or she sometimes had to use the doors to open jars, and any time something creaked outside her window she hated to be the only one checking to make sure nothing was outside waiting for her.

No. She wasn't lonely. She was just tired of being alone.

Giving up the pretense, she let all the anger and tension ease out of her shoulders. Her spine curved forward, and she leaned closer to the faerie, who reached out a hand.

The little fae patted Morgan's forehead. "You don't have to be alone all the time," she said. "It's okay to want people around."

"I don't want people around. I don't even like people."

"Then why don't you have faeries? You seem to like us, and we like you."

Morgan wished it was that easy. She would love to have a garden full of faeries like this one. They could pollinate all her flowers. Little mud monsters could ensure the soil was healthy, and the plants were getting enough food. Hell, she'd even take a couple Arcane's just to have snakes eating her mice.

"I wish I could," she replied. Sadness made her voice thick and quiet. "But witches and faeries don't mix."

"Why not? We mix well enough here!" The faerie darted up into the air, spinning in the moonbeams. "We could live together forever! Wouldn't that be perfect?"

She gave the faerie a tiny laugh. "Because witches need to live in the human realm. We're immortal, like you, but only with the sacrifices we make in our own realm."

How many things had she killed? Too many to count, although Morgan was unlike the others. She tried to sacrifice smaller animals to the world, taking their life force as her own.

A rabbit gave her five years. A deer, maybe ten, unless it would have been killed by a wolf early in its life.

Something dark in the wells of her magic bubbled to life. The young men had given her over four hundred years combined. Morgan would remain alive for a very long time.

And that's why witches sacrificed humans. They just lived longer.

Shivering, she rubbed her arms to clear the goosebumps from her skin. "No, I'm sorry. I can't stay here. I need to go home, and I can't. So I feel trapped."

The faerie floated back down in front of her, a frown on her face. "You can't go home?"

Morgan pointed to the places where portals would open. "The Mountain King said these only open on Imbolc and Samhain. I can't leave this place until then. They're months away."

A blinking, blank expression washed over the faerie's face. Morgan's gut twisted. Why was the faerie looking at her like that? As though Morgan had said something it didn't understand?

"How did you get here?" the faerie asked.

"Another faerie opened a portal for me. They wanted me to kill the king, that's is why I tried when I first came here."

"Oh," the faerie said. A bubbling smile brightened her face. "Then just do that again!"

Again, an icy shiver trailed down Morgan's back. A warning, perhaps, that she was about to open Pandora's box. "I can't. Remember? The king said the portals only open on Imbolc and Samhain."

The faerie heaved a sigh. "Yes, those portals only open on Imbolc and Samhain. But why don't you just have another faerie open you a portal? We can do that whenever we want. The king doesn't trap us here."

Her heart stopped beating. Her lungs stopped taking in breath. And her stomach dropped out of her torso and far into the earth below.

Any faerie could open her a portal?

The damned king had lied to her. No, not lied. Twisted the truth, and she had believed him!

Morgan licked her lips and asked the faerie one more time, just to ensure she had heard correctly. "So any of you could open a portal for me?"

"Well not any of us."

Morgan's rush of anger eased.

The faerie continued, "Only the bigger ones. Portals take a lot of blood and magic to make for someone your size. I can open one for myself, but you'd only be able to fit your arm through it!"

There it was again. The rage made her hair stand on end and every bit of her witchcraft boil inside her.

He'd lied to her. He'd made her feel like she was trapped, stuck, enchained. And for what?

Did he think he had trapped a pet witch? That she would stay here, sucking in his magic and every other bit of him? Like a slave he'd taken from the human realm, as he claimed faeries loved to do?

Her power stretched deep in her belly. It spread through her bones, strengthening her with all the magic of ancient witches burned at the stake. She heard them screaming in her head. He'd taken her freedom, just as they had experienced all those years ago. And they would make him suffer for it.

She stood. The frame of her body felt stronger, filled with a power that was all her own. Electricity crackled at her finger-tips. Her hair moved in a wind that did not blow.

"Witch?" the faerie stammered, her voice quiet and hesi-tant. "Did I say something wrong?"

Morgan stared at the creature, and she could feel heat behind her eyes. Her voice warped with hundreds of other witches, so angry they came through in a scream that echoed through the gully.

"No. You did nothing wrong."

The faerie bit her tiny nails. "Why do you look angry then?"

"Because I am, little one." She turned back to the forest and felt the tree roots recoil. "I am furious."

Morgan strode toward the forest and the cottage beyond where the Mountain King slept. Where he had stolen a kiss and some of her magic.

If it took a large faerie to open a portal for her, then she would drain him dry.

15

R age crackled underneath her skin. She floated down into the valley, her feet barely touching the ground. The pools of her magic burbled like a cauldron ready to pop.

All she could focus on was that he'd lied to her. And for what? A few weeks where he had toyed with her, forced her to absorb his magic, and then this?

He could have sent her home. Liam didn't need to keep her around for any reason other than to satisfy his own natural curiosity, or his own need. She didn't care what the reasoning ended up being. She would show him why no man should ever try to trap a witch.

Morgan threw the door open with a spark of magic flung from her fingertips. The solid wood hit the wall this time, not the floor.

A whispered word sent the pots in his living room ricocheting to the sides. They remained unbroken, but the plants screamed their discomfort. She hadn't hurt them, just woken them from their slumber.

Her ears rang as Monstera roared inside her hidden room.

The rage in the plant's voice threatened retribution if the witch tried to kill her master again.

Morgan didn't have to take his life. All she needed was enough blood to open a portal and then she would leave. She'd disappear from their lives forever.

But first, she wanted to ensure their king remembered never to trick a witch. Ever again.

The door to his bedroom creaked open. He stood in the doorway, peering at her with a sleepy gaze. Shadows clung to his form from the darkened room beyond. She could just make out the long tangle of his hair and the broad set of his shoulders. Loose linen pants covered his legs, but he wore nothing to keep his bare chest from her hungry gaze.

He should have quaked in fear. Morgan hovered in the air, her toes just touching the ground. Her hair whirled around her head. Her eyes burned with anger. White hot electricity crackled between her fingertips and she swore thunder rolled in the distance.

"You lied to me," she growled. Hundreds of voices laced with hers. The age old anger of women who had been repressed, lied to, and made guilty for existing. Witches whose ashes lived inside her lungs.

"Faeries can't lie, Morgan."

"But you can twist the truth. You trapped me here!" Her words snapped with power. A tendril of lightning shot off from her fingertips and hit the ceiling. A shower of sparks rained down upon them.

At the threat, he narrowed his eyes. "Careful. You've already broken more things in my house than I usually allow. If you break more, I won't be responsible for my actions."

"Is that a threat?" She almost hoped it was. Then she could unleash her anger without feeling the slightest bit of guilt.

He stepped out of the bedroom and into the dim moonlight. He was too beautiful for her to look upon, and that made her even more angry. The chiseled shadows of his abs caught her attention even through the haze of anger.

She wanted to lick her tongue between the valleys just to see if he tasted like honey there as well. The damned man had clawed his way into her head, and she wanted him out of it.

Another pop of lightning hit the ceiling near him. This time, a single spark fell onto his linen pants. The burst of flame wasn't her intention, but she felt an answering flare of power from him. He hissed out an angry snarl and slapped at it.

"Morgan, stop this."

Even more power built inside her, pouring out in waves of wind that pushed him back. "Tell me to stop it again."

He looked at her through his shield of long hair. "Stop what you're doing now, woman."

The order rolled through her very soul. Let him try to control her. She'd show him why he should fear a witch.

Lifting her hands, she let the power roll from her fingertips. It sank into the ground and the pots all around them shuddered, clanking and popping. "Stop telling me what to do!" she shouted, and her voice echoed.

Roots reached from the ground, shredding the floorboards into splintered pieces. They tangled around the king's legs, forcing him to kneel.

The potted plants grew impossibly fast. Their stems stretched up into the air, then coiled around his arms. More and more reached for him even as he snapped off their vines.

Morgan flicked her gaze to the ceiling. The moss on his roof grew long roots that tangled in his hair, pulling and creating a webbing that held him in place.

More greenery grew quicker than he could break free until the king was trapped within his own creation. His own realm rebelling against him until he was kneeling at her feet.

Again.

She stepped toward him. Her hips swayed in a loose walk of confidence. A descendent of witches had bested him.

Morgan knelt and tucked a finger underneath his chin. She forced him to look up at her. Power swirled in her belly, desiring nothing more than to be released into him. She wanted to play havoc in his mind.

But now wasn't the time for that. Instead, all she did was smile. "I said I'd kill you, king. It just took me a little longer to get you back on your knees."

To his credit, he didn't appear concerned about her words. Instead, he allowed her to tilt his head up and exposed his throat. "Please, witch. If you came here to kill me, you wouldn't have made such a racket."

Was he not afraid? He should tremble at the sight of such power before him. She frowned. "What is it you think I came here to do?"

"You came back to finish what we started."

"Of all the arrogant fools," she snarled. "You lied to me. You could have sent me back with a portal at any point during this entire charade. I don't take kindly to prisons, Liam."

He licked his lips, and the small glimpse of his pink tongue made her knees weak. "The sound of my name on your lips is foreplay enough. You didn't have to bind me, witch."

Morgan pulled her hand back from him as though he had burned her. How dare he turn this into something sexual! She wanted to go home. He was her ticket there, and he would send her back. Whether he wanted to or not.

She reached her hand out and a small pruning knife shot to her palm. She caught the handle and shoved it underneath his chin. "I'm afraid we don't have time for games, handsome."

A spark burst to life in his eyes. A green spark she recognized all too well.

She shouldn't have talked so much.

"Life's a game, witch," he growled. "Checkmate."

The vines holding him in place snapped. His arm shot out and wrapped around her, yanking Morgan against his chest before she could even blink. The pruning shears dropped to the floor with a dull thud. His heat burned her palms against his heartbeat.

"Let go of me," she berated, her entire body shuddering with pleasure at the feel of his smooth skin against hers.

Liam leaned down and inhaled her scent. He followed the column of her neck with his nose, breathing deeply as he held her with arms made of iron bars. "You're still wearing the dress I put on you."

She continued to struggle against him. "What else was I supposed to wear?"

"I can think of a few things." He leaned back just enough to grin down at her. "But I'd prefer nothing."

She bared her teeth in a snarl. "You have high hopes for tonight, faerie."

Long fingers skated down the open back of her dress, tracing the ridges of her spine. "Oh it's more than hopes, witch. You came back to my home just when I hoped you would."

"I didn't come back to sleep with you!" A burst of power rocketed down her fingers and sank into his muscles.

His torso twisted away from her like she'd tasered him.

Good, let him feel a little of her bite. She wrenched herself out of his arms and stumbled backward. Even then, her entire body yearned for him. She wanted his fingers on her back again. She wanted them on her breasts, between her legs, even one in her mouth.

Damn it!

She pointed at him, electricity still dancing between her fingers. "What have you done to me?"

He opened his arms wide. "Nothing. I could ask the same of you, but I realized a while ago you weren't casting any spells on me. I can only believe we feel the same. I'm just not fighting it."

She was absolutely fighting whatever was between them. He was perfection incarnate, and she needed to protect her damned soul.

Breathing hard, she took a step back into the rubble of his living room. "I don't want you."

"Yes, you do."

"I want to go home," she gasped.

He followed her across the tangled roots now dormant on the floor. "No, you don't."

Swallowing hard, she bumped against the wall and pressed her back against it. "I don't want to ever see you again."

Liam braced his arms on either side of her, caging her between muscular forearms. He leaned down and whispered in her ear, "Your lies taste like whiskey."

Shit. He was a faerie. He knew every time she lied.

Morgan didn't even know when she was lying. But she knew in this moment, she wanted nothing more than him. His skin on hers. His taste in her mouth and his passion pouring into her like a bottle of sangria on a frigid winter's night.

She thudded her head against the wall and whispered, "Fuck it."

Wrapping her arms around his neck, she pulled him flush against her body with the force of an avalanche. The hot thrust of his tongue sent shock waves straight to her core.

She moaned. The sound wrenched from her body without permission, but he reacted like he'd been waiting for it. Liam groaned against her lips and palmed her thigh. He lifted first one leg, then other, pinning her against the wall with his hips.

He was already hard and hot between her legs, pressed exactly where she wanted him.

Just his touch was like she'd dipped herself in lava. He warmed her to the bone when she hadn't realized she'd been freezing.

His tongue traced her lips. He lingered at the corners of her mouth, licking and tasting her. He was equal parts rough and tender, both man and beast.

She muttered against him, "This means nothing, faerie."

He lapped at her words, sipping them into his body like the whiskey they were. "Are you changing your mind, witch?"

"Would you let me?"

At her words, he stilled. Liam pressed his forehead against her collarbone and the gusts of his breath fanned down her chest. He took a few moments before responding, "If you change your mind, then I'll let you walk out of this cabin. Whatever impression you have of the fae, we don't force women."

It was enough. More than enough for her to place a hand against his neck and squeeze. "Then continue, faerie. But don't disappoint me."

She could feel his smile against her wrist. He turned and pressed a kiss to her pulse before easing them to the floor. His firm grip prevented her from falling. She felt light as air in his arms.

He helped her lay back on the floor, cushioned with soft moss. Morgan lifted a brow.

A prideful grin spread across his face. "Comfortable?"

"I might have preferred the floor."

He rolled his body, pressing his hips, stomach, and chest against hers in the briefest of touches that had her arching into him. "Trust me. You won't."

His head dipped down, lips tracing the outline of her shoulders. Warm and soft, they trailed up to her throat, only to follow the line down to her collarbone and between her breasts. Morgan's breath caught as his tongue flicked out and eased under the fabric covering her breasts.

She lifted her hips, impatient for more, but his palm landed on her hip and pushed her back. So he thought to be in control? She'd fight him for that.

But for the moment, she didn't want to. He had shifted the fabric aside, and his mouth was so close to her. His hot breath fanned over her nipple until she couldn't stand it.

"Liam," she moaned. "For god's sake."

"God?" he chuckled. "I thought witches weren't a fan of the guy."

He sucked her nipple into his mouth and then all she could focus on was the warm, wet heat of his tongue flicking back and forth. She arched again, and this time he let her.

His hands trailed down her sides, easing the fabric of her dress up her thighs. Each handful of fabric let cool air tangle around her legs. But it felt good. She was burning, aching, and she needed the chill to contain the desire.

Morgan shook her head from side to side. She desperately needed him to touch more of her. Not just the incredible talent of his mouth and the grazing fingertips on the outside of her legs.

His mouth shifted to the other side, sucking, flicking, warm again but not enough. Not nearly enough.

With a rough groan, she took matters into her own hands. Morgan locked her legs around his waist and twisted. She thought perhaps he hadn't expected the sudden movement because he rolled with surprising ease. Liam's head cracked hard against the ground as they rolled off the mossy bed and onto the hard, knotted roots of the floor.

She straddled his waist and pressed down against the hard, feverish heat of him. Reaching up, she grabbed a handful of his long hair. She wrapped the length of it around her wrist and forced his head to the side.

Morgan grinned down at him. "You're fucking a witch, not a faerie. I don't do gentle."

She dove for his mouth, nipping at biting at his plush lips. Too soft, too full. Faeries were always made of soft things and gossamer threads, so beautiful and yet so delicate.

He groaned, dark and masculine. Morgan reached between them and palmed his length. He was scorching and hard, almost too thick when she'd only experienced human men. Not a single one could measure up to him.

Rotating her hips over him, she let out a breathy sigh. She'd been right. He would ruin her for all everyone else, in more ways than one.

She dipped her fingers underneath the waistband of his pants. Her fingertips grazed his velvety head, only to be ripped away as he lurched upright.

Liam caught her around the waist, tugging her hard against his chest and pinning her hands between them. "That's fine then, witch. Rough it is."

His other hand caught her wrists. There was no fighting his grip as he lifted her arms high above her head. Green magic flowed from his body, pulsing through hers and shooting up into the ceiling.

Vines stretched down above her head and tangled around her wrists. They held her in place and no matter how hard she tried to free herself, they remained locked.

She tilted her head back to survey them, then looked back at him. "Shackles?"

He leaned down and licked one of her nipples. "For now."

Liam eased back down until he laid flat on the floor. Then the roots rolled. They moved him down between her legs until his face was right where she wanted him most. His fingers stroked feather-light up her thighs until he tongued her core.

She threw her head back again as stars burst behind her eyes. He didn't just kiss, he ravaged. No inch of her was left untouched. His tongue swirled through her slick wetness. His lips closed around her clit, and he sucked.

At the same time, he fed her a burst of power so strong it overflowed her magic. Green light danced behind her eyelids and she shattered. Burst into a thousand pieces only to be brought back by the soothing lap of his tongue as he eased her down to earth.

He trailed kisses up her legs to her hip. The roots shifted again, bringing him up her body so he could lay a kiss against her cheek. "Ready, witch?"

Ready for what? She was liquid in his arms.

Morgan still nodded. She held her breath as he lifted his hips and pushed down his pants. Just enough to free himself.

His blunt head pressed against her core, nudging but not enough. Not a thrust, not anything more than just the barest of touches. She tried to ease down on him, but the vines still held her in place.

She let out the tiniest moans, a sound of frustration and need. "Liam," she gasped.

"Do you need something, witch?" He taunted her. Pressing into her just a bit and then retreating.

Morgan's eyes snapped open. She glared at him and snarled, "I'll do it myself then."

The overwhelming amount of power he'd fed her made it so easy to order the roots to move. They jolted him up toward her and he sank root deep into her soft folds.

Every thick inch filled her to the brim. Her eyes rolled back in her head. He was perfect, every throbbing inch.

When she could think again, she opened her eyes to stare at him. His beautiful face, blush staining the peaks of his cheekbones. His head tipped back, and those plush lips parted, slightly moving as though he muttered a prayer.

Perhaps he did. The experience felt rather godly to her as well.

He opened his glowing green eyes and met her gaze. "The roots, witch."

"What of them?"

"Let me move, woman."

Right. She released her magic.

The instant the roots moved back from them, he palmed her hips. Slowly, he moved against her. Drawing himself out almost entirely before thrusting back inside her and grinding.

She hissed out a long breath, then reached for his hair again. She wrapped it around her wrist and used it to draw him closer. Their lips locked together. Holding onto his mouth like a lifeline as he plunged inside her.

Morgan hadn't known it could be like this. As if he'd clawed his way inside her with every single twist of his hips.

Magic shed off them in waves of green energy. Falling like leaves and landing in sparks on the ground.

He grunted, moving faster. Rougher. Harder inside her until there was nothing but the two of them. Just him and her until she came. All her muscles locked, squeezing down upon him while her thighs shook.

Liam gave one final thrust, pushing so deep she swore she felt him in her soul. His groan was like music in her ear. He shuddered, pulsing deep inside her body for long moments before he finally relaxed.

The vines released, and she slumped onto his chest, breathing hard while staring at the wreckage of his cabin.

The entire living room was a field of flowers. Tiny veins of green magic danced along their petals in ever moving sparks. She didn't know what kind of flowers they were, almost as though they'd created something new.

He smoothed a hand down her slick back. "Not bad for a witch."

Morgan grinned against his shoulder. "Well, you weren't all that bad for a faerie."

"All that bad? I was perfect."

He was, but she wouldn't feed his ego. "You were just fine."

"Fine?" He stiffened. "I need to remedy that."

Her eyes filled with tears. Not because she was overwhelmed, but because she knew what she had to do now. And it wouldn't be easy.

"Soon," she whispered. "For now, why don't we rest?"

"Morgan..." His brows furrowed with worry. He reached for her cheek and caught a tear on his fingertip.

He'd given her so much magic, it was easy to flex her powers. She poured a sleeping spell into him, and he wouldn't think a thing of it. After all, they had just spent so much energy. People slept, cuddled up in each other's arms.

"Rest," he murmured, eyes glazing over and worry forgotten. "Yes, let's do that."

She waited ten heartbeats until his breathing was even and deep. Then Morgan reached out and sliced his wrist with her last remaining fingernail. Just enough to pour onto the ground and let a portal shimmer to life.

Morgan untangled herself from his limbs and situated her dress. Once covered, she stared down at the sleeping faerie. Even nude and in repose, he was an artist's dream.

She pressed a kiss against her fingertips and blew it at him. "I don't think I'll forget you. If that's any consolation."

Then, she stepped through the portal and back to her lonely life.

16

———

The portal sent her hurtling home. She focused on the little cabin in the woods where she could finally feel like herself again. The only place where she was completely and utterly safe.

What had she done? Sleeping with a faerie king, Heaven and Hell, she was an idiot.

She knew what faeries did. They sank underneath human skin, poisoning sane minds until they were addicted. She'd need his touch, his scent, even the sound of his voice. And then where would she be?

Nothing more than a faerie slave, and she'd seen them before. Morgan had met so many of them it made her heart ache just to think of those poor women.

She wouldn't turn into one of them. So she had to leave. Coming back to the real world was the only option. Staying in his faerie built realm would be the end of everything she knew. It would be the end of her, and she wouldn't suffer through knowing she could have left and didn't.

Now, she needed to focus on how to get around the

strangers who'd blackmailed her. And the coven. Oh, she hadn't thought of the coven.

Morgan landed on her hands and knees in the middle of her cabin. She needed to hide from so many people now; she didn't have time to think of any faerie man. Good. It would all keep her mind busy.

She lifted her hands and stared down at the black smudges covering her fingertips and palms. Ash?

Dark, inky ashes covered her hands and knees. They ruined the white dress she wore and made the air smell like charcoal.

Brows furrowed, heart in her throat, Morgan looked up at the wreckage of her home. Someone had come into the cabin and burned it to the ground.

Tears flooded her vision. Her plants, her beautiful vines were nothing more than black charred pieces hanging from the ceiling. Her hammock was ashes on the ground. Smoke stains covered the walls and holes revealed even her garden had been ruined. All the plants plucked up from the roots and left to die while she was in the Mountain King's realm.

Their ghosts screamed in her mind. They called out for their mother, but she hadn't heard their screams of pain and anguish. She hadn't been there, and she should have been there.

Morgan let out a sob that turned into a wail of rage and anger. How dare they?

Who would step foot into the home of a witch and burn it to the ground?

Green magic swelled in her chest. She had so much of the Mountain King's magic in her. She hadn't wanted to use it, he could track her if she did, but there was no choice.

Morgan slapped her hand into the ashes and growled out a spell. "Mother moon, oracle of lunar light, send to me your second sight."

Sparks of power danced down her fingers. The shock wave lifted all the ash into the air, then pounded it back into the floor. Moonbeams sliced through the cabin like headlights, blinding her.

She kept her hand on the ground until the cabin looked as it had when she left. All her plants hanging from the ceiling and in the window. Wind rustling the leaves outside. A song dancing through the hedgerows, sang by the leaves and the roots tangled in dead boys' hair.

Her door banged open and three laughing men strode through. They held beer bottles in their hands.

"Is this supposed to be the witch's hut?" one of them asked. He was taller than the others with a shock of red hair pluming like bird feathers from the top of his head.

"Yeah," the brunette replied. He was short and squat, but stronger than the others. "Tommy used to say she was the prettiest woman in town, but I've never heard of a witch who was pretty."

"You've heard of witches before?" the last one asked. He was the attractive one. Handsome features, square jaw, blonde hair slicked to his skull. "Witches ain't real, man. We might as well just burn it."

The tall one was poking around in her pots. He lifted a rat carcass by the tail. "You see this shit?"

They shouldn't be searching a witch's cabin if they didn't want to find things that terrified them. She watched them paw through all her things. They trashed the place, leaving whatever they found on the floor as if someone didn't live in the house.

Rage boiled in her soul. They thought they could just violate her home like this?

It was the pretty one who found the first proof of witchcraft. "Yo! Look at this satanic shit!"

Her book of spells. Every coven member had one, and every spell was more dangerous than the last. She hoped they poked too much and whispered the words that would raise a demon.

If a demon burned her cabin to the ground, at least she could force them to rebuild it.

But the young men didn't whisper a spell. Instead, they found something much worse.

The short one dumped her chest onto the floor and then swore. He lifted out a patch of a jersey, one they recognized as their own. "Isn't this Tommy's?"

All her sins were coming back to haunt her. They became enraged as they realized the missing boys from town had been here. In this cabin.

They threw their beer bottles and shattered the glass against the wall. Alcohol made them stupid. They didn't care what they wrecked as they spent their anger on her home.

Morgan flinched as they ripped her vines apart. She gasped as they broke her pots and windows.

But it was the ghosts of her plants that hurt her heart the most. She could hear them calling out to her. Begging for her when their dirt had already gone dry.

Where was she? Where was their mother?

Jaw shaking as she held in the tears, she squeezed her eyes shut and let the vision fall from the cabin. She sat in the ashes of her home, in the place where she'd once felt safe, and cried.

This was supposed to be her haven. All she wanted was to be left alone. Why could they not leave her alone?

"Well damn." The voice cut through her grief like a knife. "I didn't think she'd actually come back, but you were right. Burn a witch's stuff and she shows up."

Every muscle in her body locked. They were still here.

The fools. Did they think they could come into a witch's home, burn it, and then threaten her? Their luck had run out.

She shifted, curling her hands into fists and holding magic deep within them. "You should have run."

Two other sounds approached. All three of them were still here. The idiots. They had no idea what they had done.

The first who had spoken, the one she thought was the short boy, spoke again. "I don't think so, lady. There's three of us and only one of you. Now, you wanna tell us what you did to Tommy?"

Oh, she'd tell them. Morgan looked over her shoulder and glared. "Tommy? Was he one of the boys who came into my wood with alcohol running through his veins? Was he one of the boys who thought they could corner me, pull up my dress and see what a witch hid underneath her clothes?"

The short boy turned red. "Tommy wouldn't do anything like that. You're lying! What proof do you have?"

Why did everyone always want proof when there couldn't possibly be proof? She was alone in the woods! No one was there to hear her scream except the four boys who would never have told on each other. There was no proof except her word and no one wanted to believe a witch.

She turned away from them and sank her hands into the ashes of her children. "The proof is in their bodies buried under my hedges. You can try to dig them up, but Tommy and his friends aren't there anymore. I devoured them. Their souls tasted like cheap beer and hotdogs."

"You bitch!"

She could smell alcohol on their breath. Their fiery anger pushed them forward with clumsy steps and an ill planned attack.

Morgan swept her fingers down from beneath her eyes to her chin. Black streaks coated her cheeks as she turned toward them and opened her hands.

Power blast forward. It caught two of the boys in the chest and sent them tumbling back. The third boy hesitated, pausing before her.

She rotated her hands, fingers spread open and electricity

crackling between her fingertips. "Like I said, you should have run."

"You killed our friends," he spat. The pretty one. The one who should have been home with his cheerleader girlfriend and a football scholarship.

Morgan tilted her head to the side, ear nearly touching her shoulder. "Oh you sweet little soul. You're going to taste so sweet."

The two others stood up. The redhead bolted from the room, running as fast as his feet could carry him. The other, the short one, stood his ground. "We'll make you pay for what you did to our friends," he snarled.

"No, you aren't. You're going to give me more years than I know what to do with," she replied. "Your friends deserved to die."

"Tommy was a good person!"

"No," Morgan shook her head. "He was good at pretending to be a good person. Those are two very different things."

She let out a bolt of lightning that caught the short one in the chest. He stood shuddering in place for a second before he dropped in a dead faint.

The pretty one took another step away from her, breathing hard. "Please, lady. I don't want to die."

"The surprising reality is that no one wants to die." Morgan felt the smallest twinge of pity for the boy.

Maybe he wasn't like the others. Maybe he had been roped into something he didn't want to do, but lacked the courage to say no. It was a shame people like him existed. He was just as much a problem.

From behind her, she heard wind as something heavy rocketed toward her head. Just before it struck, she heard the third boy, the one with red hair, say, "Don't hurt him!"

Something struck her head and Morgan saw only darkness.

17

Groggy, Morgan tried to open her eyes. Her head pounded. Her lungs sucked in air, but she didn't remember what had happened. Why did she feel as though she'd been in battle?

Eyelids lifting, she stared through the shadows into the room beyond.

She was in a small fishing cabin. Fishing rods and lures hung on the wall in front of her. She laid on a bundle of loose rope. The rough hemp dug into her bare back where the dirty dress gaped open. Her left leg was asleep and both her arms were tied behind her back.

Tugging on the rope proved she was tied quite well, although it also brought all her memories back. They might be stupid little boys attacking a witch, but they knew how to tie someone up.

She tried to move quietly so they wouldn't realize she was awake. Not yet, at least. She wanted to have a few more moments to survey her surroundings.

There was only one door into the cabin, and it appeared

only two windows. She didn't turn her head just yet, but that was her escape plan. She'd walk out those doors in about two seconds.

The boys just didn't know it yet.

Keeping a witch in one place was a tough task, reserved for the best assassins. Usually, if a coven wanted to attack another witch, they sent someone who was the complete opposite in magic.

These three fools didn't know what she was capable of. They'd seen a bit of her magic, but they knew nothing about witches. They only thought they'd caught one.

She whispered out a minor spell and felt the rope at her wrists fray, then release.

She didn't pull her arms forward, not yet. The boys still had a lesson to learn. First, she would gut them. Then, once they had fainted from pain, she would drink their souls and enjoy their lives for another three hundred years.

She wondered if they'd taste the same. A bit of boyhood was still left in them, that always tasted like pond scum. A bit of man in them, that was more earthy and wood-like. Then there was always the guilt, the feeling that they deserved what they got, that tasted like bile.

She'd gagged after eating their friends. They hadn't tasted good, and she hadn't eaten a human in a very long time. The two didn't mix all that well.

"I think she's awake," one boy muttered.

"Nah, she's just shifting in her sleep."

"Sleep?" She heard the rough sound of palm over hair. This one must be the redhead who had struck her. "I don't know man, I hit her hard."

There was the guilt. That one would be particularly acidic. Oh well, she'd keep him down and the taste in her mouth would dull once she ate actual food.

"Good! She admitted to killing Tommy and the other boys. You know the entire town spent days looking for them and all we had to do was go into the woods?" That must be the short one. He seemed like the ring leader.

The first boy who had spoken, the blonde she assumed, replied. "Why do we even have her here? We should give her to the police. She admitted everything to us, like you said. That's gotta be enough to put her in jail."

Yes, that was a lovely idea. No human jail could hold her. She'd show up at their windows in the middle of the night, scratching at the glass so they knew she wasn't finished with them yet.

"Because the police won't do anything! She's just going to lie to them and then we'll be in the same place as Tommy and the boys." The short one was correct. Maybe he was smarter than she gave him credit for.

They would keep arguing if she let them, and she was tired of sitting on the rope.

Morgan shifted more obviously and let out a theatrical groan.

All the boys stopped talking. They even held their breath if her hearing was correct, before one of them stood up. Considering the heavy steps, she had to guess it was the redhead. His footsteps were unfamiliar. He'd run too fast for her to guess what the sound of his movements were like.

He knelt in front of her. A thousand freckles dotted his nose. She would have thought him cute if she didn't know the darkness lying in his soul. "We've got you all tied up, witch. There's nowhere for you to run."

"You're such a sweet, innocent boy," she whispered, lies flowing from her tongue like wine from a bottle. "Why are you doing to this to me?"

He cleared his throat. "Look, lady. I don't want to hurt you. None of us do. Why did you have to go and kill our friends?"

"Is that what this is?" Morgan wanted to poke a bit. For curiosity's sake. "You want revenge?"

The redhead wasn't like the other two. The short one wanted to hurt people, she could see that in his eyes. His tall, handsome friend was merely a follower. But this one, he had a mind of his own.

If she pulled at his soul just a bit more, he'd reveal so much more.

Morgan released a tendril of magic through the floor. It wrapped around his ankle and underneath his clothing. The tiny spark of light would wiggle into his heart and soon he'd tell her all the things he didn't want her to know.

She asked again, "Do you really want to do this?"

The boy shook his head, eyes glazing over with green magic. "No ma'am. I don't want to hurt anybody and I feel awful bad I hit you on the head like I did."

"Hey!" A shout echoed behind her. "What are you doing to him?"

"Nothing," she murmured. "I just want to know if I should kill him."

The redhead shook his head, trying to clear the magic from his mind. "I don't want to hurt anybody, Tony! I want to bring her to the cops, like Craig said."

"Shut up, you idiot! We're not bringing her anywhere. We're ending things now."

Morgan reached forward and touched a hand to the redhead's face. She cupped his cheek and watched as he curved into the heat of her palm.

Flashes of his life filled her mind. He was a respectful boy who lived alone with his mother. She worked too much, so he tried to do the man's role in his family. But he was just a child, and he didn't know what he was doing.

Being around these two made him feel more like a man. They were puffed up with ill begotten pride. Every action they took made him feel more and more uncomfortable, but now he'd told them too much. They knew his mother liked to inhale white powder and that sometimes she hit him when he disappointed her. This made him less of a man. A woman overpowering him made him nothing more than a little boy. Didn't it?

"Sleep," she murmured.

He dropped to the floor like a stone. She let him fall. A few bruises would remind him not to mess with witches in the forest.

She stood and turned to the boys at the back of the cabin. They both stood next to two chairs and an empty fireplace. No lights were on in the cabin, but that was better for her.

The blonde looked at the door, then back at her. She snapped her fingers and pointed. "Don't move, Craig."

"H-How do you know my name?" he stammered.

Well, no one said they were bright. They had just heard their friend say their names, hadn't they?

She could scare the boys into wetting their pants, or she could take her own revenge. Morgan wasn't sure which one seemed more attractive to her at the moment. The screams of her dying green children still echoed in her mind.

Tony, the short squat one with a black soul, picked up a metal baseball bat that had been leaning against a chair. "Fine. We'll finish this now."

"What do you think you're doing with a bat?" she chuckled. "I'm a witch, sweetheart. That won't do anything to me."

He reached up with his free hand and pulled out a necklace. A cross swung from the end of the chain. Gold and glimmering in the dim moonlight, it cast light beams all over the room. "You can't touch me. I have God on my side."

She grinned. "That's very cute. But God and I don't talk much. We sorta have a deal. He turns a blind eye to magical creatures and we don't tell you how many things live in the shadows."

Craig turned pale. "You mean, there's more of you?"

Time to frighten the boys, she supposed. They were foolish and dumb, but perhaps they could be turned away from being so dangerous. Her revenge would be sweeter if it lasted throughout their lives, and besides, she still had four hundred years to live herself.

"Everything you've always feared, they're real. Witches. Vampires. Werewolves. All the stories humans tell are from truth. I'm sure your parents don't believe in any magic, but I can assure you. It's very real."

Tony scoffed and tightened his grip on the bat. "Sure, lady. Whatever story you want to tell to scare us, you can try. But we'll still get revenge for our friends."

She let some of her power melt into the room. It chilled the air until every exhale fogged. They might not even feel the cold just yet, but it was an effect she was going for. They should think she was terrifying and shiver down to their bones with the knowledge they'd come across something impossible.

"You can try to hold something like a shield, Tony. It won't help." Morgan flicked her fingers, and the bat went flying.

It struck the wall with a clatter and fell to the floor. The boys stared at it with wide eyes.

A part of her felt guilty. They were just children who thought they were doing the right thing. It made sense, in a twisted way.

Their friends were dead. They'd caught the killer and had been raised on stories where children could kill villains. Harry Potter, Artemis Fowl, even Percy Jackson. All children who bested the bad guy.

But that didn't happen in real life. Sometimes children were caught in the web of an evil person.

Morgan took a single step toward them and grinned as they retreated. "What were you going to do to me?"

She sent tendrils of power out and wrapped them around

Tony's throat. They sank into his vocal cords and forced him to tell the truth. "I was going to convince them I wanted to kill you, but first I was going to finish what Tommy started."

"Which was?"

"I wanted to make you scream," he growled. "I don't care how. If that meant doing what Tommy wanted to do, then I was going to do it."

He couldn't even say the word rape. She dug into his mind and found the word itself was so vile to him, he didn't even want to think about it. So he justified actions by pretending they were a punishment for evil people instead.

"Get out of my head." Tony's eyes were wide and wild. "Why can I feel you in my head?"

"It's an unnerving feeling, isn't it? To have someone else inside you without permission."

"This isn't the same thing." His words were frantic, but his body couldn't move. She wasn't letting him. Not yet.

Craig moved to the corner of the room, pressing his back against the wall and shaking in fear. "Please, lady. Let us go."

"Were you going to let me go?" she asked, turning her gaze to him. "Or were you going to watch me bleed out because your friends are dead?"

"You said you killed them," he whispered, his voice shaking. "What else were we supposed to do?"

Listen to her? Understand she had no choice but to protect herself, and sometimes safety ended in blood? Humans were fragile. They were so easy to break.

She'd always tried to be kind to them. To understand that humans lived in a unique world, surrounded by a protective bubble that shielded them from creatures of the night. She stayed out of their way. She didn't want them anywhere near her powers or her person.

Morgan tightened her control over Tony, who struggled to

get free. She pushed deeper into his mind and found out he'd been bullied as a child. This had made him mean because if he was stronger than the bullies then they'd leave him alone.

But that darkness had sunken into his soul. Now, he enjoyed hurting people. Too much.

"You never meant to hurt that girl," she whispered. Power flooded her vision in a veil of white. "You could taste the blood on her tongue after you hit her. But you hit her too many times, didn't you? And your father covered it up because he's important in town. The mayor, is it?"

"What are you talking about?" Tony growled.

"You knocked out three of her teeth because she made you angry. Your father paid for surgery and her parents are absent, so they didn't care. But you liked it. You'd do it again." Morgan could feel her own teeth loosening as she relived the tragic moments. "That's why you wanted to hurt me. You want to see if still feels good to make women scream."

"Get out of my head."

Craig shifted further away from them both, closer to the door. "Tony, what's she saying man? I thought Angie fell?"

"She did," he growled. "This bitch is lying."

Morgan stood so close their noses almost touched. "Witch. Get it right, Tony."

Craig bolted out the door and into the night. That was all right. He'd tell people of a witch, but she couldn't go home, anyway. He was just a kid.

This one... He wasn't a child at all. Not anymore.

"There's a darkness in you," she told him. "I can feel it. It's spreading through your body like a cancer."

"Get away from me."

"No," she muttered. "I don't think I will."

Out of the corner of her eye, she saw a shadow over the window. Morgan thought maybe the blonde had returned, so she diverted her attention away from the man with the wicked soul.

It wasn't a person standing outside the window. Vines shattered the glass and crawled through the window moments before the entire room exploded with green magic.

18

Liam desperately tried to see through the haze of emerald coating his vision. The green magic inside him boiled so hot his skin felt as though it might peel off. He didn't know what was underneath if the magic finally succeeded.

He'd tracked her all the way to this fishing village full of disgusting humans. How, he wasn't sure. Something inside her called out to him. Something familiar to him.

He could feel her deep inside his chest. His own magic didn't call to him, but her magic did. It bubbled like liquid silver, deep in his belly. He'd touched it with his mind as he traveled, rolling it like a worry stone.

The thought of her leaving him for someone else enraged him. The elemental wanted to rip out of his physical form and devour their souls. How dare they touch her? How dare they think a human was worthy of her love?

The dingy window hid many details from his sight, but not all of them. Someone *had* touched her. He could smell the blood in her hair and could see the rope burns on her wrist through the glass.

He let them talk; he listened to their words and even stepped out of the way as the blonde man ran past him. He'd get the boy later. A burr had stuck to the boy's pant leg, and he'd find it was impossible to remove.

If the Mountain King wanted to find a human, he would do so.

But then he'd heard the words the other one said. The one who threatened Liam's witch. The boy who wasn't a boy at all, but a young man coming into an adult life full of hatred and anger.

He heard the threat on the man's tongue. How he had intended to hear Morgan scream and the Mountain King finally agreed with the elemental magic within him.

Humans were filth. They had destroyed the human realm and now they wished to destroy the woman who he valued more than anything.

If this boy thought destruction was his power, then he was about to meet a faerie who could do so much more.

Green magic flowed off him like a deer shedding its antlers. Vines crept in through the glass windows, shattering them and absorbing the sharp shards. Thorns grew all along their lengths.

The boy gave a frightened scream. Good. He should feel fear when he witnessed genuine power.

More vines grew out of the ground and twisted down through the chimney. They reached for the boy whose death would be too swift. With one final pulse of magic, Liam released the elemental to do whatever damage it wished.

He only vaguely heard Morgan's frightened scream. Didn't she know the magic wouldn't hurt her? It wouldn't touch a single hair on her head. Both he and the elemental agreed.

She was precious to them.

Eventually, the magic drained. The elemental was appeased and retreated into the safety of Liam's mind. It wouldn't return for a while, now that it had finally feasted. He hadn't allowed the creature out for a very long time. Even in his own realm, it had only the briefest hints of freedom.

He'd let the elemental do whatever it wanted. He feared what destruction he would find in the shack.

Liam couldn't see through the windows anymore. Vines and roots tangled in place of the glass. Knotted and gnarled, they glistened with red blood.

He picked his way over the land that rolled with more plants than a forest, all in a single space. He made his way to where the door once stood and waved a hand. The roots released their locked position and allowed him into the shack.

The boyish man was frozen in the back of the room. Roots and vines impaled his body, at least thirty in just his torso. Thousands of tiny spikes poked through his arms and neck. He was barely alive, just enough to gurgle in fear as Liam strode toward him.

He stood before the man and shook his head. "There are worse things in the world than a witch. You shouldn't have touched her."

He turned away from the sight, disappointed in humanity all over again.

Memories flickered to life in his head like lightning bugs coming out at dusk. He'd left this place in disappointment of what humanity had become. They destroyed, they maimed, they hacked away at the world. They didn't appreciate it.

Liam had felt the burn of hatred in his heart. All those years ago, nearly a thousand now, and he still felt the same way. He was still so disappointed in the creatures who had the ability to do so much and instead, they just ruined everything they touched.

Far away from him, Morgan knelt on the floor. She covered something with her own body.

He approached and realized she'd created a cage of vines,

protecting something from his magic. Glittering sparks surrounded whatever she'd kept in the cage.

Shockingly, the elemental awoke. He waved a hand with its overwhelming magic, and the roots released their hold. Beneath them, one of the boys laid asleep. His stark red hair glowed in the moonlight.

Perhaps she didn't want to hurt him. He understood the guilt of taking a life such as the boy's, but it was the same as killing a sapling so the rest of the forest could flourish.

Liam lifted a hand but froze when Morgan said, "Stop."

"Stop?" He furrowed his brow. "Why would I stop? This is the one who hurt you. I can smell your blood on his hands."

"But he didn't want to." She held her hands over his body as though that would prevent Liam from killing the boy. "He deserves to live. He still has a chance."

"A chance for what?" She should want revenge on the boys, shouldn't she? Kill them. He didn't care. "He's human. They're expendable."

Morgan met his gaze with large, watery eyes. "No. Not this one. If there's a chance he can do something right, something that will improve the world, we should let him."

"There are a thousand more exactly like him, living in the precise circumstances." Liam waved his hand and the roots around the boy lifted like snakes, ready to strike. "Losing one will change nothing."

"I said stop!" Her voice rang through the room with the promise of power. "Let him live, Liam."

He needed to understand the mercy she was willing to give these children. Liam crouched in front of her, ducking his head to stare into her beautiful eyes. "Why? Why this one?"

She reached out and smoothed a hand over the boy's forehead. "I looked into his soul and I saw something bright there. Something rare."

"What will he do then, oracle?" He knew the word would

sting her, but there was some truth to it. She'd seen his future when she touched him. He knew because he'd seen it as well, through her eyes and his magic in her soul.

Her gaze watched the boy as he slept, but Liam could see Morgan had disappeared. She slipped into the magic of her mind and he felt the answering tug deep in his belly.

She used his magic to see the future, and he could not be more proud.

"He's not a remarkable person. His future is one with a quiet life. A pretty wife who's very shy, but he helps her out of her shell. A little boy with red hair who becomes a mechanic in this town. Neither leave much, but they're kind, and they like to watch football together on the television."

Liam snorted. "You see? Entirely unremarkable. Take your revenge and his life."

She pulled herself from the future. "No," she said. "The world needs more people with quiet lives. He lives."

Liam wanted to argue with her more, but he could see she wouldn't budge. This boy was worth fighting for, at least in her opinion. And in this moment, he could deny her nothing.

He sighed. "Fine. Whatever you wish, witch. He lives."

Morgan reached out and touched a single finger to the boy's forehead. She pressed down hard on his third eye and whispered a spell Liam couldn't hear. He could, however, feel the tug of magic.

He followed it into the mind of the boy who dreamt of a carnival with an older woman who smiled at him. Somehow, he knew the smile on the woman's face was rare. The magic dug into the boy's memory and erased everything from this day. She smoothed the edges of sharp memories where the smiling woman had hit him and coated his mind with softer words.

Only then did Morgan sigh and release her hold on the boy. She listed to the side, catching herself on a root.

"Morgan," Liam reached for her. He helped her stand on shaking knees.

"I'm fine," she whispered. "That's just a lot of magic. A human mind is hard to manipulate, but I managed."

His chest puffed with pride. She'd only been able to do all this because of him. She'd taken magic from Liam and used it to do wonderful things. Even if one of those was saving an insignificant human.

He pulled her to his chest and squeezed her, perhaps a little too hard. He pressed his mouth to her hair and whispered, "Sweet witch of mine, I feared the worst when I followed you through the portal."

"How did you know where I was?" She murmured the words against his chest.

"You've got my magic inside you. I can find you anywhere." And he would follow her to the end of the earth, even if she insisted on fleeing from him. Soon, she would learn she couldn't run far enough to free herself from his presence.

Then, to his great surprise, Morgan wrapped her arms around his waist. She let him take her weight and relaxed in his hold. He hadn't ever thought to be so blessed.

Her complete trust made his heart swell five times larger than it was. The elemental in him sighed. Green magic glowed from his chest, passing into her and refilling whatever pool of magic she kept in her mind.

He was only mildly insulted she thought of magic outside his element. Water wasn't nearly as powerful as earth. His own store of magic was a majestic tree, stretching roots throughout the realms.

Someday, he would train her to think of her magic the same way. Together, they would weave green magic through this world and strengthen it.

Together, he trusted they could heal the human realm. Whether the humans remained in it or not.

The man's body was still behind them. He could hear the creaking of roots trying to hold the weight in place and not drop him to the floor. Liam couldn't leave it there. The redheaded boy would awaken to see his friend hung up like some kind of strange voodoo doll.

Liam flicked his fingers, and the roots moved through the earth. They dragged the man deep into the belly of the ground where he would remain locked in roots forever.

Now that the body was taken of, he needed to get Morgan out of here. If the redhead woke up, she'd have to wipe his memory again, and that had taken its toll on her. She pressed herself against his chest as though he were the only thing keeping her standing.

Liam took a step back. Her knees buckled, but she held herself up straight.

Pressing a hand against his chest, she muttered, "I'm fine."

"You're not fine," he replied. "Let's go."

Morgan took a step away from him, standing on her own two feet. "I'm not going back to your realm. My place is here. I can't go back to some made up world."

He hadn't intended on bringing her back to his realm where she was uncomfortable. However, he was curious. "Why not?"

She gestured around them. "This is where I belong."

He looked at the ruined fishing shack. "It's a little plain."

"I don't mean here here." She shook her head. "I mean in this realm. This is where I belong. With the humans."

"They've nearly destroyed this place. If my magic isn't the end, then they will ruin this place on their own." He stepped closer and held out his hand. "But if this is where you want to stay, then for now, come with me."

She eyed his hand like it were a viper waiting to strike. "There is good in humanity. I know you don't see it, but they are fighting to keep this realm alive just as others are trying to destroy it. I was wrong. You were wrong. We must find the good ones and believe in them."

"Do you really believe that?" The mere idea was fascinating to him. Humans were weak creatures, fragile and so easily manipulated. He'd never thought of them as anything other than pawns in a larger game of life.

"I do," she whispered. Her eyes opened wide as if her own words surprised her. "I don't think I used to believe it. But I have to hope they will spread their kindness throughout this world."

"Why do you believe that?"

"Hope is a dangerous thing," she replied. "But it's all that keeps us immortals alive."

He supposed she was right. He still had hope for his old home in the faerie realms, even though he knew it existed only in battle and hardship. Perhaps he could spare a little hope for this place as well.

Even if he still thought humans were nothing more than destructive, insignificant creatures with limited minds.

"Perhaps the humans will surprise us," he said, then wiggled his fingers. "Now, let's go somewhere safe."

"Safe" appeared to be the magic word. She slipped her fingers into his with no hesitation. He let the green magic take over his mind again. And together, they allowed the roots of the earth to rise over their heads and pull them somewhere safe.

19

She'd never traveled through the earth like this. Portals were easier for those with magic. This was just roots taking them through the ground to an unknown place.

Morgan had never even thought magic could do this. But then again, the Mountain King had surprised her so much.

She thought she hated humans more than he did. And yet, she still repeated the words the strangers had told her when all this started.

Humans are an important part of how the world runs, we cannot let them all die.

She hadn't agreed when the vampire had said the words. She would have been the first to say humans were beyond saving, and anyone who tried to help them was wasting precious energy.

Now, Morgan thought she might have been wrong. Not because the boys tried to get their revenge. Not because yet another person had died for her.

But because she'd seen into their minds. She had seen the little redhead boy and the love overflowing from both his parents.

She'd never felt that kind of love, or even tried to feel it through a human's mind. Not in all five hundred years of her life. And she was stunned by its power.

The world needed humans for that reason and that reason alone. Immortals and magical creatures were so stingy with their emotions. Love wasn't something most immortals believed was even real.

Humans felt love with their entire being. They gave it freely, and without need for it to be returned. The gift of love was in abundance in their world. They loved their pets, their homes, each other, and all of that was magic only they could give the world.

So she wanted the boy to live. She wanted that magic to be cast out into the world, even if that meant it only fell onto the soil around his little farmhouse with his quiet wife. The ground where he lived would always show them fair harvest. Their kitchen stove would never break, and their boy wouldn't fall and break an arm. No spell she ever cast was that powerful in comparison.

Roots warped around her and opened up to reveal a little room like the one Liam had made for her in his realm. Vine woven walls and a roof made of leaves tangled around three tree trunks. The floors were woven branches that could hold their weight high above the ground.

They'd be safe here. Safer than she was in her old home, though there was nothing left for her there.

Morgan sank down onto the bed of leaves and moss in the corner. She sat on its edge, staring down at her hands, and wondering what had changed.

Why did she feel such mercy now? Why was she capable of these thoughts when her entire life had been focused on ignoring them?

Liam settled next to the window, his eyes watching the outside world. "What happened? I saw them talking to you about other young men and I felt the remains of their energy in your hedges."

Morgan shook her head. "That memory is not for you."

He turned his gaze to her, burning anger once again making his eyes glow. "What did they do to you?"

She met that angered gaze and said, "I don't want to tell you."

"Will you ever?"

"No."

He watched her for a few more moments before giving her a sharp nod. He turned his powerful gaze to the window once more, and the tension drained from her shoulders.

She couldn't talk about that night. If she did, then she would have to tell him about the countless other times she'd been abused by men, women, humans. All the times she had been cast aside as a witch.

She'd tried very hard to not let her history make her into someone she wasn't. Morgan had forced herself to overcome the anguish and hardship of rejection. She had sifted through memories of hatred and pain.

Five hundred years was a long time to process being alone. But somehow, all those years didn't make it any easier.

The hole in her heart was a hard one to fill. It was even harder to admit it existed.

"So this is what the human realm looks like now," he murmured.

He watched the outside as though it were a puzzle he couldn't figure out. In all the dramatics, Morgan had forgotten he hadn't been here for centuries.

She watched him. His eyes darted in all directions, soaking in whatever details he could. His hands closed on the edge of the window, squeezing until it creaked.

"Yeah," she replied. "I'm sure it's very different from what you remember."

"There are so many lights." Said lights were reflected in his eyes, tiny stars dancing over his features. "How does anyone sleep with so much light everywhere?"

"We just do."

"How do you even see the stars?" He looked up at the sky. "There used to be so many more stars there. Did the humans kill them as well?"

"No," she said with a soft laugh. "They're all there. The lights of the cities just compete with them."

He grunted. "It seems a rather bleak way to live. The stars were the prettiest part of the human realm."

She hadn't even thought the brightness of stars in his realm was surprising. She'd stared up at the Milky Way every night and never had a second thought or wondered that she could finally see it.

Morgan sighed and laid back on the moss bed. "I always stayed in my cabin, so I could see the stars."

"Is that a shooting star?" He leaned out of the window and eyed something moving across the horizon. "It's moving very slow."

Her mind stalled out for a second, trying to figure out what he was seeing. She was so tired. Standing up to check the sky seemed like too much.

Then she realized what he was looking at. "Is there a blinking red light?"

"Yes," he muttered. "It's very strange. When did stars turn red? What have the humans done to this realm?"

Morgan rolled onto her side and cushioned her head on a hand. She yawned and replied, "That's not a star, Liam. It's a plane."

"A plane?" He turned to her with a raised brow. "I have a feeling that doesn't mean something flat."

Another yawn forced its way out of her mouth. "No, I'll

explain it in the morning. We might need to take one eventually if the coven is hunting me down."

"The coven?" he asked.

But sleep was already claiming her. She wanted to explain to him there were dangerous things likely searching for her. That she needed him to look out for witches on the horizon.

She drifted off into sleep with dark worries rampant in her mind.

Her dreams were strange. She stood before a council of people. Not just her coven, but the strangers who had arrived at her house. They all pointed at her and claimed she hadn't done the right thing. That she was a failure because she hadn't killed the king, but also because she wasn't a good witch.

Though she begged on her knees for forgiveness, her coven and the strangers still called for her death.

The rest of the night she spent running. From her past. From her people. From everyone she had once trusted.

Morgan awoke in a cold sweat. She froze, listening intently for the sound of another person in the woven room. But all she could hear was the sound of crickets.

She eased up onto her hands and searched for the faerie king who had saved her. When she realized he wasn't in the room, she leaned down and pressed a hand against the floor.

"Where is he?" she asked the trees, and they hummed in response.

"Outside," they sang. "Out the window."

Why, of all places, was the Mountain King sitting outside the window?

She crawled out of bed and stumbled to the vine made window. The Mountain King sat upon a canopy of leaves, a picture in repose. Branches had created a netting beneath him so he didn't fall. Leaning back on his hands, he stared off at the city. His brows were furrowed in thought, his lip between his teeth.

She wondered what he was thinking. Was the world so different these days he recognized nothing?

Just cars probably blew his mind. Let alone all the other things that had changed. In a thousand years, humans had created so much. Infinitely so, and likely in terrifying ways.

Morgan climbed out the window and picked her way across the treetops to join him. He didn't look at her as she settled down next to him.

Wrapping her arms around her legs, she put her chin on her knees and watched the city with him. "Is it overwhelming?" she asked.

"In some ways. These are strange new creations you humans have placed into the world."

"I'm not human," she reminded him. "I watched this place grow and change more in the past five hundred years than in all the centuries put together."

"They adapt quickly." His expression changed to one of immense worry. "And they destroy so much in a short amount of time."

There it was again. His inevitable hatred of humanity, something she hadn't realized was so ingrained in his soul. She knew he was angry about the state of the world. Who wouldn't be? Green magic had died out so much here that it was almost nonexistent.

But he couldn't blame the humans. Though they tried to be better, they would always hurt something with their new machines.

Still, she believed their capability to love would save them. More than the immortals could.

"Why do you hate them so much?" she asked. The question was as quiet as the rising sun.

His sharp inhale made her chest hurt. It was the sound of heartbreak and old pain that rose to the surface before he could stuff it back into the shadows.

Liam rubbed the back of his neck. "When I was a young fae, I thought it smart to come here. To the realm of the humans with another faerie who I was most interested in pursuing."

She smiled. "What kind of faerie was she?"

"She was from my brother's Summer Court," he chuckled. "A scandalous love interest considering I was born to lead the Spring Court. But she was beautiful. A water nymph with a heart of gold."

"She sounds lovely." A pang of jealousy struck her chest, but Morgan reminded herself she had no right to be jealous. The woman was no longer in the picture, clearly. And he was a faerie. They had more partners than they had memories.

"Every bit of her was lovely, so much so she made mortal men weep just at the sight of her." His hands flexed, turning into claws. "I don't know why they killed her. Only that they thought perhaps it would serve them in some way. They took something beautiful and because it was different, they decided she was terrifying."

Morgan didn't want to know how they'd killed a faerie. Back then, they would have thought of her as a demon who could destroy their families. The nymph would not have had a quick death.

She shivered. "So that's why you hate them."

"I don't hate them." His gaze narrowed upon the city. "You can't hate beings that are like insects. Even worse. They are a stain upon the world and all they do is spread their disease."

Morgan reached out and took his hand in hers. She linked their fingers together, tightening her grip until he had to look at her. "I thought the same, but after looking into that boy's mind... What is the one thing immortals cannot do? Or at least easily?"

He frowned. "I don't know. Immortality provides many ways to succeed."

"Love," she whispered. "Can you honestly say in all your

thousand years of life that you've loved something? So much you'd be willing to die for the person?"

Liam's gaze turned heated, warming into something she'd never seen before on his face. He squeezed her fingers in return. An answering pang twisted in her heart.

He shook his head. "I don't know."

"They do." She pointed toward the city. "They love their animals, their cars, their family and friends. All of it spills out of them and feeds the magic of this world. Their lives are so short, less than a heartbeat to us. But they love more than we do in a thousand years."

The words were poetic, but true. Humans were necessary because immortals couldn't feel the way they did. Hundreds of years dulled the heart and the mind until love seemed so far away. So out of reach.

He turned back to the city, staring at it as though the flickering lights were suddenly more important. A puzzle he couldn't figure out. "Maybe so," he murmured. "Does that outweigh the bad?"

"I think so." That's why she'd saved the boy. His future might not be earth shattering or cancer saving. He was still important, though. And that's what mattered most.

Liam sighed. "Either way, we can't stay here. I called a friend who's letting us stay in his home for a while. In the city."

"A friend?" Surprise lifted the hairs on her arms. "Who do you know in the city?"

He didn't look at her. Something was different today. Something strange and ominous boiling underneath his skin.

Liam took a while to respond, and when he did, it was nothing more than a brief shrug. "I might have disappeared from this realm, but my court didn't. The Spring court remains."

Why did that make her stomach tighten in fear?

20

Liam let the elemental take control to ease them out of the tree. The magic it used was almost beyond him.

There was no spell. No flexing of power. Just the knowledge that whatever it wanted, it would get. Sometimes, he wished he lived life as the elemental did. Other times, he wondered if its selfish ways were a curse.

Morgan remained quiet until they got to the ground. She glanced around them, then back at him. Nerves made her eyes darker than normal, although he couldn't tell if she was uncomfortable or just worried for him.

"I'm fine," he told her, reaching out and placing a hand against her back.

She was warm against his palm, supple where most women might have been weak. Her body had been made strong by years of witchcraft and hiding from the rest of the world.

"I'm not sure I am," she replied. "Liam, listen. I didn't go to a witchcraft council. The coven will be looking for me. I've probably been labeled as some kind of outcast witch and they don't suffer to live."

"Let them hunt you then." He shrugged, even though the

elemental raised its head deep within him. They both wanted a fight. It sounded like more entertainment than taking on the humans she pitied so.

"I don't think you understand what that entails. The witches hunt together as a coven."

He slid his hand up her back to her shoulder. Tugging softly, he tucked her against his side and walked them through the forest. "The faeries will help you, Morgan. Let the coven try to test their might against my people."

"Starting a war is the last thing I want to do between the magical communities."

"Then perhaps they won't hunt a hedge witch who lives alone in the forest." He pressed a kiss against the top of her head. Her hair was soft as silk against his lips, and the strands smelled like mint. "You might be important to myself and my people, but the coven of witches may overlook your transgression."

She shuddered under his arm. "Witches aren't all that likely to forget."

Then it was a battle he'd fight for her. He didn't know why, but her words had stuck in his mind.

When was the last time he had fallen in love with someone? Well and truly fallen in love?

He couldn't put his finger on the time. The nymph killed by humans had a special place in his heart. She was a wonderful creature, a breath of life in this forgotten world. But had he loved her?

He hadn't felt the way he did for Morgan. This woman made him want to break things. To shatter the world just to ensure she was protected, even though he also knew she could protect herself.

Liam had found himself infatuated with many things. Never for very long, however. His attentions shifted in so many directions, especially when he was younger.

This woman held his attention at all times, however. Just the way she moved was like watching her dance. Her words were poetry, though he rarely understood her meaning.

Love.

The word burned in his mind. Why? He wasn't certain. He knew what the word meant. So many people claimed to have felt it in their lives. The emotion plagued humans and poets for centuries.

He helped her over a fallen tree trunk and guided them away from the destroyed cabin. The elemental sent out a few tendrils of magic to make sure the boy she wanted to save had left. He had. The tinge of sweaty fear still clung to the roots.

Now, he just had to get them somewhere safer. Somewhere no one but his own people could find them. The Spring Court were the only ones he could trust these days, it seemed.

"Where are we going again?" she asked.

A smudge of dirt streaked her nose. Her clothing was equally soiled, but he couldn't do anything about that right now. He licked his thumb, then cleaned it off the tip of her nose before responding. "One of the faeries has a house in the sky."

"A what?"

He tried to remember what the faerie had said when he reached out. The pixie had been shocked to hear the Mountain King in his head, but he'd been most helpful.

Liam hadn't reached out to any of his court for a very long time. They ran mostly without his intervention, although sometimes he would invite visitors to his hidden realm. The Spring Court was filled with well behaved creatures, though. His counterparts weren't so lucky. The Autumn Court in particular needed an iron fist to rule.

Shaking his head to clear the memories, he replied, "A house of pent, I believe he called it. In something that cuts the sky."

Her eyes grew round as dinner plates. "Someone in your court has a penthouse in a skyscraper?"

"Yes, those are the word."

"Wow," she muttered. Morgan stepped ahead of him, guiding them toward the road with confident steps. "Who knew the Spring Court was doing so well in the human realm?"

"They like to fit in."

"Apparently so." She stood next to the dirt road with her hands on her hips. Morgan surveyed left and right before turning back to him and asking, "How are we getting there?"

He wanted to speak the same way she did. His vocabulary was lacking in this realm. The words sounded like they were English, but they didn't move the same way on his tongue.

Liam reached her side and searched for something that might resemble a "car" or whatever it was his faerie had stated. "They were sending someone to pick us up. That's what he said."

"Gotcha." She cocked her hip to the side and placed her hands on her waist. "Well, I guess we wait then."

Liam wasn't a patient man.

He reached out through the root system connection he had with the entire Spring Court. In his mind, he connected with the pixie once again. "Where is this ride you spoke of?"

"They should be there any moment, my king."

"And what precisely am I looking for?"

"A silver Charger, Your Majesty."

As if those words meant anything to him at all. A charger was a horse, but he had a feeling that wasn't the case. Humans had changed too much since the last time he'd been here.

He missed his own realm. The simplicity and quiet was all he desired out of life.

A rumbling sound down the road caught his attention. Dust plumed before the metallic beast, hurtling toward them with surprising speed. Considering Morgan didn't run from the beast, he assumed it was acceptable to remain where he was.

Still, he closed his hand into a fist and gathered a ball of energy. Just in case he needed to protect them.

Morgan glanced over her shoulder at him. "That's what your faerie sent, I assume."

"It is."

The silver "car", as the humans called it, was terrifying. It moved with wheels instead of legs. And when it stopped, the dust plumed around it like the entire thing had snorted.

Liam didn't want to touch the beast. A chariot would have been far more efficient and easier to drive. Where were the horses? Why would anyone choose this over what had worked for centuries?

Morgan started toward the car without a backward glance. She opened its side and stepped somewhere beyond his sight.

What in all the faerie realms had she done? Did the beast eat her?

Her head poked back into view, and she gestured for him to come with her. "Come on, faerie king. Get inside and it'll take us where we need to go."

As if he wanted to be eaten by a creature that coughed toxic poison into the air and gleamed in the sunlight like armor.

He frowned at the car, but supposed there was no other choice. Liam had to get to the city with this woman. He had to know what it was like to be human, because the elemental within him was curious. It wanted to know what else the humans had done to their realm.

Why? He wasn't confident.

The elemental had always known its purpose. End the human realm and the suffering of the planet they were destroying. But there were always other options, other paths they could take.

In his heart and soul, he'd always thought they would

destroy the human realm. What else could they do? The humans didn't listen to reason. They were foolish creatures who never understood what pollution could do.

Morgan thought otherwise. So, with the hope of love in his chest, he got into the belly of the creature that would deliver them to this house of pent.

He jumped when the beast growled as soon as he shut the door behind him.

Morgan chuckled. "It's just the engine."

"Humans have created monsters to do their bidding for them, then?" he asked.

She reached out and took his hand in hers. Her fingers twined with his helped ease his anger and fear. Liam felt strange knowing that such a simple connection could soothe his torment.

"The humans have created many wonderful things and many terrible things. Just like us." She squeezed his fingers, and everything was fine again.

He didn't know how to reconcile that. Fine? Nothing could be fine when he knew coming back to the mortal realm was a task waiting to be completed. The elemental would eventually take control again and he wasn't in his own little realm where its magic could run rampant safely.

If he lost control here, then he would destroy everything in his path.

So many sights flickered past him on their ride. Everywhere they went was something new. Cars like this one in all shapes and sizes. Buildings that stretched up into the clouds. People wearing clothing that was far more revealing than he ever remembered humans being comfortable with.

He saw tiny objects in their hands that they stared at with complete confidence. Lights that told them when to walk and when to stop. Food on every corner in so much abundance he wondered how they weren't all overweight.

They lived with so much around them. Pictures in the sky that changed colors and moved like giants lived among them. The humans didn't even look up, however. They just kept staring at the objects in their hands and ignoring life.

Liam didn't notice he'd pressed his nose against the window until he moved back. The smudge on the glass was embarrassing enough. Let alone his expression. He must have been open mouthed and drooling.

"It's okay to look," Morgan murmured. "A lot has changed since you've been here."

She had no idea. All these changes were overwhelming and not enjoyably.

There were no plants. Nothing was left in this hunk of metal other than a few green specks on porches that were badly cared for.

He could hear them screaming. There was something called a park nearby, at least that's what the trees said. They were manicured until they couldn't even breathe. They wanted to be wild and free like their cousins. They called out for his help, but he knew he couldn't do anything.

He needed a distraction. Something that would take his mind away from all the horrible things happening here. He wanted to believe the humans could be good. He wanted to believe they were more than what he had always thought.

Distraction. Anything.

Liam turned toward Morgan and asked, "When are we seeing this house of pent?"

She leaned forward and asked the faerie in the front seat, "How much longer?"

"We've arrived, Your Majesties."

"Oh I'm not-" She didn't get the chance to finish her words.

The metal beast stopped, and the faerie in the front seat got out. The side of the beast was opened, and the faerie stood to the side as he awaited the king's exit.

This, Liam was comfortable with. He knew the court system like the back of his hand. The faeries should bow to him. He was their leader, but more than that, he housed the spirit of spring within his chest.

He wished he could explain to Morgan how the faeries worked. While the coven might vote in their leader, faeries respected only power. And there had always been the same power in the chest of each and every king.

But he wasn't supposed to tell anyone about the creature inside him.

He stepped out of the car, and a blast of stale air hit him in the face. It smelled like gasoline, trash, and the ever present odor of metal. He coughed, pressing his hand against his mouth and nose to somehow preserve his lungs.

They lived in this? The humans lived in a city where the air was killing them?

Morgan got out of the car and stepped up to his side. "Come on," she mumbled, lacing her fingers with his once more. "Let's get inside."

The faerie who had been driving them dropped into a low bow. Then, surprisingly, he reached out and caught Liam's free hand.

No one of the court touched the king without permission. Liam frowned down at the young fae until he realized the creature was desperately trying to send a message through their mental connection. He was still very young and needed physical contact to speak through minds.

Liam allowed access only to wince as a scream blasted through his mind.

"Save us, Your Majesty. We've suffered in silence all these years as the dying plants screamed for our help. We are outnumbered, but now that you're here, we can rebuild the earth."

The faerie released his hold and ran to the front of the

metal beast. It started once more, the grumble of the engine roaring as the faerie guided the beast away from them.

Save them?

Had the boy been asking for the Spring Court, or was he speaking on behalf of the trees? The grass? The forgotten places buried under miles of concrete?

Morgan tugged on his hand, guiding him toward the front of the entirely glass building. "Let's get out of the street, shall we? I know this is all new for you, Liam. I don't want you to get overwhelmed."

He was more than overwhelmed. He was angry.

The humans had destroyed something proud and grand. He could feel the spirits of the plants that had once been here. The forest that had stood tall and noble until man had walked among the trees and thought they would be better as furniture and houses.

He could feel every step of the centuries. Every moment when the trees had been hacked and destroyed. Their screams were sown into the earth like a tapestry of pain and anguish.

His ears rang with their screams until he could hear nothing else.

Morgan dragged him through a doorway. Cool air eased the heat of his cheeks. It smelled better in here, but not by much. Cucumber and mint assaulted his senses. She forced him to move to the front counter where a salesperson stood, or maybe a guard. He couldn't tell anymore.

"Hello," she said. Her voice eerily polite in a way he'd never heard her speak before. "We were told to stay here by a friend. There should have been a note for Liam..." She glanced back at him.

"Liam MacCarrick," he murmured. He'd always used the same name in the human realm. Hopefully those in his court remembered his preference.

The man at the counter frowned at him, then looked

through a stack of papers on his desk. "Here you are. Penthouse suite! Lucky woman."

He scanned something plastic that reeked of poison and handed it to Morgan.

She took it with a sweet smile. It looked fake on her face, and he wanted to wipe the expression off her lips.

Frustration grew as she ushered him into a metal box that moved on its own. At least this he understood. Magic was far more familiar than all the technology staining this place.

Pressing her back against the wall, she heaved a lengthy sigh. "There we go. That's over and done with."

Over and done with? He wasn't nearly over and done with whatever he'd seen outside. The human realm needed to be cleansed.

She must have seen the thought play across his expression. As the metal box beeped, and a door opened to reveal a room beyond, she reached for his hand and held it against her heart. "Liam. Whatever you saw out there, I can explain it all to you. I can prove they're trying to stop whatever effects you might have felt on the planet. Just give me time."

He didn't have time. The world didn't have time. It was screaming, and he couldn't help but listen to its call.

Still, he let her guide him from the metal box into the cool room beyond.

Most of the walls were glass. A lower level appeared to be a seating area with white couches and chairs very low to the ground. A metal fireplace crackled, providing warmth to an otherwise sterile environment. The kitchen, although he thought such a place was only for servants, consisted of black cabinets and white countertops.

Perhaps the wall of windows might have been appreciated by the humans. He could see all the glistening surfaces of every tall building ruining the sight of the trees he knew were some-where beyond them.

"Liam." Again, her voice cut through the red haze of his vision. "You're raining flowers."

Not flowers, seeds. He stared at the maple tree seeds drifting in the surrounding air. They looked like faeries. Wings helped them float through the air and glide to new places.

Perhaps he would lose control again. Maybe he would make trees grow throughout this building until the humans were choked, just like they had done to the plants.

No, he needed a distraction. That had been his plan, and Morgan wanted him to listen to her. To believe for a few moments that he was more than just an elemental or a king ruled by his own hatred for humans.

He would be a good man. He would be a good king.

Unfortunately, those two plans seemed at odds.

Desperate, he reached for her. Liam tunneled his hands through her hair and pressed his lips against the soft cushion of hers. "Witch, I am overwhelmed. Distract me. Own me. Ruin me if you must, but do not let me look at this cursed land any longer."

She didn't respond. Instead, she wrapped her arms around his shoulders and pressed her body against his. This, he knew. The world could melt away for a few moments in her arms.

21

———

Morgan couldn't even guess what was going through his head. But the moment the seeds started flowing off his shoulders, she knew something was very, very wrong.

He couldn't lose control here. Far too many people's lives were in the balance. Why hadn't she realized this would be too much for him?

Because she'd trusted his court would guide their king. Foolish woman that she was, she'd thought faeries would understand their ruler. But they didn't.

Faeries were selfish, tactful creatures. If the king wanted to wipe this planet clean of humans, the rest of his court must as well.

If he needed a distraction, she was happy to provide it. After all, it felt as though the fate of the world was in her hands. This man could destroy everything she knew the world to be.

Morgan kissed him in a frenzied bid for passion. Though, it didn't take much to light the fires between them. He licked her lips as though she were made of sugar, and every inch of her body reacted.

She arched. Perhaps that was what he was looking for, or maybe he was just waiting for permission to use her to satisfy his own need.

With a guttural groan, he wrapped an arm around her waist and pulled her tight against his chest. His other hand twisted in her hair. She was locked against him, incapable of moving and forced to endure the fiery sweep of his tongue.

His body was solid, like the rocks of his mountains. Almost too hard, too hot, too unbearably demanding.

She whimpered as he drew her closer, pressing the stiff length of his arousal against her hip. She knew intimately what he could do with that. And while they'd both been busy, she hadn't forgotten the passion and desire in his touch.

"Morgan," he groaned into her ear, "please tell me this infernal place has a bedroom."

"A bedroom?" she chuckled, wiggling against him. "Since when did we need a bedroom?"

At that, he pulled away from her. A curious expression changed his face, softening it into something close to a smile. Liam eased his hand from her hair and stroked his thumb over her cheekbone. "You deserve a bed, witch. Not just a quick fuck on the floor of a place neither of us know."

Heaven and Hell, why did he have to claw his way into her heart like this? Why couldn't he be satisfied with using her and that being the end of it?

"Come with me," she said. Taking his hand, she led him into the back of the penthouse where she assumed a bedroom awaited them.

Her guess was correct. The first door she opened revealed a massive king sized bed with white sheets. In fact, everything in the room was white. The walls, the floors, even the dressers.

"This will not do," he muttered behind her.

Morgan felt the swelling of his power long before he used it.

The cool breeze of his magic brushed through her hair and teased her skin with electric goosebumps.

She shuddered, closed her eyes for a second, and when she opened them, the room had changed into an oasis of green. Vines dripped from the ceiling like garlands, flowering with great white petals that showered down like raindrops. Moss covered the floor and ivy tangled around the bed, creating a four poster look in what had once been a modernized beauty.

He had created a bedroom full of green things for them. A greenhouse in the middle of a concrete jungle.

She didn't get a single second to breathe out her wonder before his hands framed her hips. He pulled her back against him, pressing his hard length against her bottom and breathing in the scent of her hair. "Will this suit, witch?"

"It will, faerie."

She turned in his arms and tilted her head back, awaiting his kiss.

He gripped her ribs, tugging her against him so sharply she lost all her breath. The sultry heat of his exhalations brushed her cheeks and mouth. But he didn't kiss her, not yet. He hovered above her, rocking his hips back and forth against hers. "You are the only thing that keeps me sane, and I don't know why."

"Witches are prone to madness," she replied. "I know how to deal with you."

"All the faerie gods smiled down upon me when you walked into my realm." He pressed his lips against hers in a butterfly-soft kiss. "They cursed you with me, however. A faerie king knows only destruction."

"You know far more than that." Morgan pressed her hand against his chest. His heart beat against her palm, faster and faster as she slid her hand down his belly and palmed his hard length. "Now prove it."

Liam let out a tortured groan. His hands grasped her thighs, catching her as she leapt into his arms. He walked them back to the flower covered bed and laid her down. A cascade of petals surrounded her, and the scent of roses was almost cloying in the air.

He made quick work of her clothing. Every garment was pulled from her body with almost surprising force until she lay naked and bare in the petals.

His gaze heated until it was almost a physical touch upon her person. "You're beautiful," he murmured. "A queen I intend to worship."

How was a woman to resist words like that? He crawled up her body and was so perfect, so warm. So much more than anyone she'd ever met before.

Liam silenced her whimpers with a kiss. His hands tunneled through her hair and spread out the black locks over the pillow.

And she couldn't touch enough of him. Morgan slid her hands along his back, his chest, his stomach. The hard planes of his body were so distracting. She couldn't think when she touched him, as though he'd lit a fire in her mind that could only be satisfied through physical touch.

When she slowed, he held her hands against his chest. "Don't stop, love."

"Liam," she moaned against his neck. "Please don't make me wait."

Another shower of petals rained down from above them. The plants shuddered at the same time he did. His entire body quaked as he reached between them and fit himself between her thighs.

The slow flexing of his hips was pure torture. Morgan tossed her head back and stared up at the flowers above them. They bloomed more and more with every passing second.

She had no words to describe his perfection. The way he stretched her nearly to pain, but so full it was exactly what she needed. How every thrust took her farther, deeper into the madness of his touch.

The deep, hidden part of her that was pure instinct couldn't get enough. She raked her nails down his back without care if she drew blood. He snarled in response, bending low to catch one of her nipples between his teeth.

Their rhythm sped up. He drove into her with single minded purpose and all she could do was chase him. He was relentless in pursuit of his goal, and she allowed him to guide her. Trusted him to know that with every glide, every moment their hips met, she was one step closer to oblivion.

"Liam," she gasped, her voice hoarse and raspy. She didn't know what the question was in her tone, or what she was asking for.

But he did.

He sped up even faster, impossibly strong and powerful with each stroke.

And then it was too much. She arched her back and rode the wave of pleasure that began in her toes and clenched through her entire body. She locked her arms around his shoulders and held on as he continued, thrusting harder and harder until he too clenched his teeth and groaned.

Her entire body felt liquified. She wasn't a person anymore, just a glistening recipient of magic and incredible pleasure.

Liam rolled to the side, his lips ghosting down her shoulder. His breathing slowed from the great gusts of breath he'd drawn in. "Witch, you ruin me."

She couldn't contain the grin on her face. "Good." Morgan tugged him closer to her side, curling into the hollow of his body. "I think I like you, ruined and all."

22

———

It was a long while before she left the comfort of their warm bed. The king still slept soundly, but her mind was restless. Something called out to her, something magical and powerful.

So, she left the comfort of his arms and padded into the living room. Morgan stood in the kitchen, barefoot and covered in nothing more than a stolen blanket.

She centered her soul, allowing her mind to wander toward the magic reaching out to her. "Yes? I am listening."

The voice appeared in her mind too easily. Almost as though it had been there for far longer than she'd given it permission. "We've been waiting for you to return to the human realm. Is it done?"

Ah, there they were. The strangers who had showed up in her home and threatened her with blackmail. If they thought to force her hand, they'd be sorely disappointed. Now, they had nothing to hold over her.

There was no home for her to return to. They could dig the boys up underneath her hedges and it didn't matter if the humans found them. Her own coven had likely disowned her.

Morgan felt confident in her response. "No, it's not done. He's here with me."

A long pause boomed louder than a drum. Then came a scream, "You brought him to the human realm?"

She winced. "I didn't bring him. He came when I escaped."

"You were supposed to kill him!"

"And when I met him, I realized you were wrong. He doesn't need to die, he just needs to understand the changes in the human realm. He needs to know they are trying their best."

The stranger, she was certain it was the vampire, growled. "He is a danger to this entire realm. You would let him wander the earth when he is so close to losing control?"

"I trust him," she replied. The truth rang in her ears. She trusted him. More than she'd ever trusted anyone else, and that was terrifying.

"Then we shall rescind our deal with your coven. Watch your back witch, many people want your head on a pike."

"I have the protection of the Spring Court, vampire. Please attack me. The king you're so afraid of would love nothing more than to meet you."

She severed their connection with a resounding pop. Green magic glowed all around her, stolen from the king as she had the last time they'd enjoyed each other's company.

The strangers had talked with her coven? Why? Did they think she was on some kind of holy mission to kill a faerie king?

"I need a drink," she muttered. If this was a faerie home, there had to be some kind of alcohol in the cabinets.

Rummaging through a stranger's belongings felt a little wrong. She still did it. What else was she supposed to do while the sun set? Sit on the uncomfortable white sofa and not touch anything?

Her fingers grazed a bottle of whiskey. With a soft, "Ah hah," she pulled it from the cabinet and poured herself a tall glass.

So many questions brewed deep inside her. The strangers wanted him dead. The faeries wanted him to destroy the humans and bring this realm back to its former wild glory. Morgan didn't think either side was correct.

There had to be another option, hidden somewhere just out of her reach. An option where millions of humans could live, while the fae still thrived.

She sipped at her whiskey and watch the sun dip below the horizon. Darkness stretched over the city and all the lights blinked to life. She wasn't sure if she even moved for hours before she heard the soft sound of footsteps approaching her.

Warm lips pressed against the connection where her neck and shoulder met. "Hello, Morgan."

"Good morning, or evening I suppose."

He cupped her hips with both hands and tugged her back against him. "Why are you standing in front of the windows as though you're plotting my demise?"

She stiffened. Had she been thinking about that while staring out at the city falling asleep? She wasn't certain. But words still flowed from her mouth and poured out without her permission. "The people who sent me to kill you reached out."

"I know." He pressed another kiss to her neck. "I felt their magic."

She swallowed hard. "They wanted proof I'd done what they asked."

"You didn't."

"No, I didn't."

He hesitated for a brief moment. His hands flexed against her sides before he asked, "Are you considering killing me again, Morgan?"

She should consider it. The human realm would be safe if he wasn't here. Or at least back in his own realm where she could pull the wool over his eyes once again. But that was wrong and she couldn't be that person.

Could she?

Morgan shook her head. "No, I can't do that to you."

He relaxed his grip. "Then why are you so upset?"

She didn't know. The answer was far more complicated than explaining the human realm to him. She wanted so many assurances she knew he couldn't give her.

That he wouldn't kill anyone in the human realm without reason. That he would control his magic when she knew he couldn't.

His magic was volatile. It ruled his body just as much as he did. And that was more deadly than his opinions on humans.

She licked her lips and remained frozen in his grasp. Morgan couldn't tell him what she wanted, and she also couldn't ask the questions that would help. Instead, all she managed was, "What would happen if you took the Earthen Throne?"

He released her. Stepping away, his footsteps backed into the kitchen before he responded. "Why do you want to know that?"

She shrugged. "Everyone's so concerned you'll do it. The people who sent me want to make sure you never even get a chance. The faeries want you to take the throne and say it's important that you do."

"What faeries have you been talking to?"

"The one your magic created in your realm." She lifted the glass for another sip, only to realize her hands were shaking. "I want to know what would happen, Liam."

"You don't need to know because I don't intend on taking the throne." His voice was clipped and short.

Morgan could just see his reflection in the glass. He stood next to the kitchen counter with his hands braced atop it. The picture of a tortured hero. He stared down at the white surface instead of looking back at her.

"I want to know," she repeated. "It's important that I do."

"Why?" he spat. "Why do you need to know something that would be the ruin of everything I am?"

"So I can help you stop it." She didn't want their lives to come to that. But if she had to prevent him from ending the world, she would.

"I don't want you anywhere near the elemental or the throne."

His reflection changed. Morphing into something she didn't recognize, a person who wasn't her Liam. Branches appeared on top of his head, twining around each other into a semblance of a crown. A glorious crown indeed, but one she never wanted to see on his head.

His skin changed into bark. His face warped into something still handsome but terrifying. A mantle of green moss spread down his shoulders and touched the ground.

He was the Green Man. The god who had inspired so many of the Celts to worship him.

She remembered the legends. She knew the stories of the earth god who could destroy with a single wave of his hand.

That was not the man she knew. Nor was it the one she might love.

Morgan lifted the glass to her lips and let whiskey burn the anxiety out of her throat. "Tell me."

He blew out a long, measured breath. "The elemental is far stronger than any faerie. Stronger than a witch or the most powerful of any magical creature. It is not one of us. But it must live within one of us."

She had guessed as much. The elemental seemed to have a mind of its own. "Why does it want to take the throne?"

"Because it hates what the humans have done. It desires to see nothing but trees and green things growing. We both agreed the world was a better place when there were no humans, only fae, all those years ago."

"You can't stop progress," she argued. "Humans weren't meant to stay in the Dark Ages."

"And the earth was not meant to howl," he retorted. "What is more important to you, Morgan? The planet you walk upon or the humans who infest it?"

She squeezed the glass in her hands so hard it creaked. "There is so much good here. I refuse to believe you've blinded yourself to progress."

"You keep saying those words, but all I've seen thus far is pain and torment." He looked at her in the reflection, meeting her gaze with emerald eyes. "We could turn the world right, you know. Then we could go back to our realm, the place I built. It could be your home too."

She didn't want to live in a made up world, she wanted to live in a real one. With real people and real problems.

How could she ever take him up on that offer? Destroy the world she was in, just to trade it for one she could change at whim. Morgan wasn't a goddess. She was a hedge witch.

She shook her head and took another sip of her whiskey. "No, Liam. I want to live in this world with all its flaws. I just wish you could see the beauty of it."

The counter creaked under his grip. She feared he might snap through the marble before he let out a long, hissing breath. "The throne would destroy mortal men, but would that be so bad? It calls to me even now, begging me to help heal all the harm that has been wrought. Who am I to deny the earth?"

"There is always another way," she whispered. "A thousand ways to right the same wrong. Why would you assume the only way to fix this problem is the path of death?"

"Then give me another way to fix this, Morgan. Give me another option that provides some kind of hope. Any kind of hope."

She wished she could. Morgan could only see two choices,

however. Death or allowing the humans to continue in this realm and figure all this out for themselves.

Magical creatures were stronger than their human counterparts. She knew how frustrating it was to contain that power and hide from the world. But perhaps it was the best option for all magical creatures. Remain hidden. Not kill teenaged boys who made mistakes and bury them in the hedgerows.

She lifted the glass and took another sip of her whiskey. "I will not turn myself into a god, and neither should you."

"If I do nothing, the elemental will devour me whole," he murmured.

His words rang true in her head, but wasn't it already happening? She could see the elemental every time she looked at him. Just being in the human realm had awakened the demon. It was only a matter of time before something happened.

She couldn't stop him or his power. She could only provide momentary distractions with her own body, but eventually he'd get bored with that too.

And therein lay the real problem. Morgan realized with shocking clarity that she was terrified he would leave her. Just uproot himself from her life as if he hadn't changed everything.

She'd let him in too much. He now lived some place deep in her soul and the lack of control made her stomach roll in fear. A cold sweat broke out over her body at the mere thought of losing her authority. Of losing herself in another person.

Hands shaking, she held the whiskey glass against her belly to still the nervous twitches. "The elemental is already eating you alive," she whispered. "Even I can see that. You cannot become a god, Liam." *Even if that meant accepting his death.*

The unsaid words hung between them.

He shoved away from the counter. She watched in the glass windows as he strode toward the door of the penthouse. Without glancing over his shoulder, he spat, "If that's how you feel, then I will return to my court. My rightful place awaits, after all."

And with that, the elevator dinged. He stepped into it, and the doors closed behind him.

Morgan's throat tightened. She tried to tell herself this was for the better. He'd go back to his own realm, and she would stay here. Where she belonged.

Alone.

23

———

He made his way out of the strange building. Hot air blasted his face like a punch to the nose. He could almost feel the bones shattering.

How did they live in this place? How did any human survive day by day when the world was trying to kill them?

He stumbled down the street toward the one place where he knew he'd feel at home. The trees called to him. They whispered of a place where all the green things grew in the city. A place where they might be cut and forced to grow as the humans wanted. At least they were alive and well.

Liam needed to be somewhere green. He needed to feel grass under his feet, not concrete. He needed to smell pollen in the air and hear leaves dancing in the wind. Anything to remind him this world was still alive.

What did she mean she needed to be somewhere real? Her words ghosted through his mind, punishing and cruel. The world he'd created was more real than this one. He'd given life to so many creatures and plants. How was that any less real than this place?

He stared up at the concrete buildings stretching up into

the sky and hatred burned in his chest. This place was the one thing he needed to fight. All wars would end if he could just destroy this realm.

Then his people could come into power once again. The faeries would take over, as they had long, long ago. They would bring this realm back to its former glory without humanity ruining everything.

A loud, blaring honk shattered his vision of the future. Something yellow barreled down the road toward him. At the last second, Liam hopped back onto the sidewalk as the metal being blasted by him.

This place was dangerous. Not just for him, but for everyone else. His life had almost been taken, and he had only stopped for a second.

The world didn't have knights and soldiers now. It had regular people being careless.

He could have died in a split second when he'd not looked where he was going. He, the Mountain King, the King of the Spring Court, could have been brought to his knees by a simple metal box.

Liam had never been so angry. Energy crackled at his fingertips, green magic that could throw roots around the car and destroy it.

The elemental didn't speak in his mind. It just poured more power into his palms. He could lose control. He could release the power and make the humans pay for what they had done to the realm which had once been a faerie playground.

Liam didn't know when he released his control on the magic. He didn't know if it was even a conscious decision. All he knew was one moment, the yellow beast charged away from him. The next, an ancient root from deep within the earth shot up and wrapped around the car.

Gnarled and knotted, it cried out in happiness at the freedom he'd given it. Though the root might have been severed, it had waited for a long time to grow again. Now, power gave it life.

It coiled around the yellow car and squeezed. A man screamed within the metal interior, but it was far too late for him. The root crushed until it had severed the car in half.

People on the street screamed and ran. They bolted away from magic.

A woman ran by him shouting, "Terrorists!"

As if that was what it was. How could humans not understand sometimes it was merely the earth coming to punish them? They deserved punishment for all they'd done. Did they not see?

Power strengthened him. He strode through the crowds of screaming people. They blasted by him, carrying bags full of plastics and disease riddled pollutants. They didn't care their water bottles were choking the planet. How could they?

All they cared about was getting from point A to point B.

He strode in the opposite direction. His shoulder caught a man who whirled but didn't apologize for striking him.

Not even politeness had remained in this world. The Dark Ages had been bad enough. Humans were disgusting back then, but this? This he couldn't suffer through any longer.

If Morgan wouldn't help him, then he would release the elemental. The being deep inside him heard and rose to the surface of his skin.

Power beyond faerie magic, beyond even a god, boiled inside him. He could feel every earthen thing all around him. Roots, leaves, trunks and stems. All of it, all a source of power he could draw upon.

And the being inside him. The one that wanted to unleash the earth's retribution upon the world.

Had his counterparts felt this? Did they understand the meaning of genuine power as it was so close to his fingertips?

All he had to do was let go. Just a little. Just enough so that the pots on windowsills above him burst and the plants stretched their roots. They grew fast, stretching up the buildings and spreading great clouds of seeds.

Soon, those seeds would plant themselves into the walls of the building. They would find whatever crack they could, grow through it, and shatter concrete. They would prove the earth was much stronger than anything humans made.

He walked confidently into the park with all the trees crying out his name. The grass reached out for him, curling around his shoes and pulling them from his feet. Trees reached down and rained leaves to tangle in his hair. Branches fell with them, twisting in long locks until a crown graced his head once more.

He felt more like himself than he had in a long time. Moss dripped from the surrounding bark, pooling into a mantle that stretched from his shoulders and slid along the ground.

The park came alive. All the trees burst into a shower of petals, flowering for a second time this year. But they didn't mind. They wanted to show the king what they could do.

Power spilled from his hands and into the earth in sparkling green waves. Not once in his life had he felt like this. He'd felt power before, certainly. How could he not? He was the Mountain King.

But this time was different. The power wasn't his, so he didn't get tired. The elemental allowed him to draw from roots. This would have taken years to drain if he'd done it himself.

The ground rolled under his feet, drawing him closer to the heart of the park. An ancient tree waited for him there. He could feel it anticipating the meeting of the king.

Through his toes, he could feel the power the ancient tree held within its roots. There was something deep inside, a secret hidden for many years.

"What do you want to show me?" he asked, his voice ringing through the park. "What mysteries have you kept?"

The elemental unfurled long wings of power. Glimmering green light outlined behind him, just slight enough for him to catch out of the corner of his eye.

A faint part of him feared what was happening. He was changing, turning into something that wasn't Liam. Something that wasn't even the Mountain King. And though he didn't know what he was turning into, he somehow couldn't process any fear.

Pollen floated all around him. The dancing dust motes were so beautiful they looked like chips of gold. He strode over a hill, and then he was there. At the center of the park.

The tree had been growing for many years. Its roots were nearly at the heart of the earth by now. Perhaps that was why the humans had never cut it. Or perhaps because the leaves of this tree were sharp as knives. It would protect itself should such force be necessary.

"Mountain King," it said. The voice was the whisper of wind through leaves, yet filled with the power of an avalanche. It rolled through him with a power he recognized as his own.

Slowly, he took a knee before the ancient being. The others whispered the Mountain King bowed to the venerable. He knew the old ways. He honored the trees.

"Ancient. Luck was with me today, for it brought me to you."

The tree hummed out a long, pleased breath. "Welcome to the forest, Mountain King. I have waited many millennia for you."

Millennia? The part of him who was still Liam balked at the words. Why had it been waiting that long? He wasn't even that old. *He should never have come here.*

Someone had wanted him to remain Liam, and he'd chosen that path. For her. For the woman with inky hair fanned out across his pillow with petals in the black strands.

Power swelled over his head. It crashed down upon the

memories and wiped them clean once again. It was just him and the power.

The tree shivered. Green magic poured out of his fingertips and into the ground, sinking deep into the dirt and flowing out to the ancient being. It heaved one last content sigh before the magic overwhelmed it.

A great crack like lightning split the tree in half. It curved, warped, and twisted around itself until the sounds finally ceased. All was quiet then, as if the entire park held its breath.

The ancient tree had become a throne.

Impressively large and wonderfully beautiful, the throne had been created for him. Great vines curved into a halo of leaves around the top, raining down the back and cushioning the seat. Flowers bloomed along the twig arms and spilled down the side. It was an impressive throne for a green king who would make the world anew.

But did he want to?

Clarity spread through his mind. He shook off the control of the elemental and stared at the throne as himself.

He knelt in the green grass with blades tangled around his fingers in loving hugs. These plants needed him. The earth itself desired nothing more than freedom from the horrible things that had been done to it.

He was the only one who could save them. He was the only one with enough power to free them from the jagged pain of humankind.

Like a tooth, he could pull humanity out of the earth's mouth and free it from the torment. All he had to do was accept his place as the Earthen King. Not just the Mountain King, but a creature who had been created to rule.

Liam wasn't so sure he wanted this. A long time ago, he would have desired nothing more than to come into power. But then he'd created his own realm, and he had learned so much about his own people.

What would happen to the mud faeries if he left? The flower fae, even Arcane, who had stayed to look over that realm?

A voice echoed in his head, deep and grumbling from the heart of the earth itself. "You can keep all those things. But first you must take the throne and protect what is yours." The elemental. Who else could it possibly be?

"And the woman?" he asked. "Where will she be?"

The elemental grumbled. "Witches are humans."

"They are magical beings just as we are. I will not cause her death." He couldn't bear the thought, knowing he could have protected her. Saved her. Done something more than just wiped out all the people she loved and respected.

"Then the witches will live. They will be the last, and I shall allow only their children with magical abilities to live. It is the one concession I will make, Mountain King."

If that was what it took, then he would take his rightful place. Liam stared at the throne, at the future awaiting him.

"Will I still be me?" he asked, his voice quiet.

"No. You will be so much more."

24

———

Morgan paced through the penthouse apartment, her footsteps pounding. She should never have let him leave. He needed her now more than ever. He'd made that very clear. And for some strange reason, her stomach ached now that he was gone.

Not a stomach ache as though she was ill. But like she missed something.

Crazy. That was a crazy thought.

She turned around and paced in the other direction, toward the sunken living room with its stale white furniture.

She wasn't attached to a faerie king. And yet, she was. Damn it. The more she thought about him, the more she remembered the details of things she didn't want to lose. The way his dimples appeared when he smiled. How his hair tangled around her fingers when she played with it.

The green magic he always used around her. Not because she desired power or because he was showing off, but because he wanted her to be comfortable. No matter what the cost.

He was a kind man to the core. That was her problem.

The Mountain King was supposed to be like every other

faerie she'd ever met. He was supposed to be selfish and rude. All faeries liked to have sex and then throw aside their new partner when something new came along.

Morgan had seen it happen to people close to her. She'd warned witches before, not to get involved with a faerie. The stories always ended sadly.

She couldn't get involved with him.

But she had.

She was already so deeply involved she missed him when he wasn't there. Her heart actually hurt at the thought of a life without him, and how was she supposed to move forward? She wasn't in control of her own life anymore, and it was all his fault.

"I should hate him," she muttered. "I should hate everything he changed and all the bits of him I love so much."

She stopped in her pacing and stood frozen in the middle of the living room. Love? She didn't love him. *She couldn't.*

Faeries weren't capable of love. Immortals weren't capable of the emotion either. She'd had five hundred years to fall in love, and she'd never done it.

Morgan had thought she was in love many times. But every single person always disappointed her, and she left. That's what she was supposed to do. Protect herself, her heart, and her life at all costs.

This one was different. And she'd let him walk out the door in a huff.

"Damn it," she muttered. She needed to go back to the realm he'd created and get him back. Or at least apologize. Or maybe try to explain why she felt the way she did.

Her life hadn't been easy. It was full of rejection and the thought of him looking at her as though he didn't feel the same way... tears burned her eyes.

She waffled and she probably always would for their entire immortal lives together. Hell, she couldn't even promise tomorrow she wouldn't bolt because her mind told her he would leave. But she had to at least try. For him.

"Okay, so let's get in touch with Aster." Morgan closed her eyes, cleared her mind, and reached out for the faerie who had created the portal into the Mountain King's realm.

It took a while for her to contact the faerie. But when she finally did, their connection snapped into place so quickly it almost gave her whiplash.

"Witch?" the faerie screamed through her mind. "Where are you? Everyone said you brought the Mountain King to the human realm!"

"I did," Morgan replied. "But now he went back to his realm, and I need to follow him there."

There was a long pause. Almost as though Aster had put her on hold until she could move to another room.

When the faerie returned, her words blasted through their connection far too loud once again. "Listen to me, witch, we only have a little time. I'm part of the Spring Court, or was, still am. Not sure how to explain it. Anyway. The Mountain King is still in the human realm."

Morgan shook her head in denial. "No. He said he was going back where he belonged."

"Yes, he belongs on the throne, you nitwit. Haven't you been watching the news?"

The news? Why would Morgan watch the news?

Foreboding turned her stomach acidic. She turned to look out the glass windows that provided her a view of the entire city. There, far below, a scene unfolded in destruction and horror.

A taxi cab sat on its side, cut in two as three people helped the driver out of the front seat. The giant root knotted around it was ancient, one from deep in the earth's belly which never should have risen again. Far in the distance, she could see the park had spilled out into the human world. Plants grew wild on windowsills and concrete buildings puffed dust where they had already begun to crumble.

Sirens screamed through the night. Fire trucks approached the park, glimmering with unnatural green light.

What must the humans think? Would they blame this on aliens or would they find out too much about the hidden magical community?

"Oh no," she whispered.

"Oh no is right. You brought him here, witch. Fix it!" The faerie hissed the words and ended their connection with a painful severing.

She was right. Morgan was to blame for all this mess. She'd been the one to convince Liam she'd felt something for him. Having sex with him in the cottage hadn't been the smartest of plans. And while she hadn't known he would follow her into the human realm, some piece of her must have realized he would.

She'd goaded him just a few hours ago. Forced him to choose a side and feel as though he were alone.

She knew how that felt. People did foolish things when they were alone and angry.

"Damn it." She spat the words at her own reflection before turning and running to the elevator.

Pounding her fist on the call button, she hit it again and again. "Come on," she muttered. "Go faster."

It felt like forever passed until the elevator dinged. Morgan ran into the compact space and frantically hit the buttons that would bring her down to the bottom floor.

She had to get to the park. She had to run through the crowds and whatever cops might stand in her way, because she couldn't let him go through with this.

Morgan couldn't even entertain the thought she might be too late. She wasn't. She would get there in time and talk some sense into this foolish man who refused to listen. He might not understand that humans were important, but he'd never been here before.

The elevator dinged again, and Morgan ran full tilt toward the glass doors. The footman out front was already holding it open for people who ran inside screaming. Morgan darted past all of them with a shouted, "Sorry!"

"Ma'am, it's not safe to go that way!" the footman shouted after her. "Stay inside!"

She didn't have time to explain it was safe for her. The magic wouldn't touch her, of that she was certain. Even if he took the throne of Earthen King, he would never hurt her.

At least, she hoped he wouldn't.

Morgan ran past the shattered taxi and the man who sat on the edge of the sidewalk. His hands were bleeding, and there was a horrible cut on his forehead pouring blood onto the concrete. But two paramedics were tending him, each increasingly more and more concerned as he told his story.

The humans couldn't process such strange things happening in the middle of a city. They were supposed to be safe in this concrete jungle. A pang of guilt made her chest ache. She had been the one to cause this. She could have stopped Liam.

He'd even admitted taking his life was the easiest way to fix the situation she was in. That maybe the world would be better if he was dead.

He'd known.

He'd known, so why had he allowed this to happen? How could he do this when he knew what the stakes were?

She ran through the crowd fleeing from the park. She darted across the streets devoid of cars or any kind of vehicle. Only when she reached the park, did she find more humans.

Hundreds of them. Police officers and firemen who stood before the ever spreading greenery and conversed with each other on what to do.

Even before her eyes, she could see the moss rolling across the ground. Grass grew atop it, making it even thicker and stronger.

"What are we supposed to do to stop that?" a fireman said, his uniform wrinkled as if he had taken it out of the wash too soon. "I got some pesticide back home but I don't have enough to stop all this."

The police officer next to him scratched his head. "Never seen anything like this before."

Of course they hadn't. And pesticide would only make this even more angry. They shouldn't even try attacking the greenery, or they would regret it. The moss would grow up and over their beings, and they wouldn't be able to stop it.

Her vision made more sense. If they touched the spreading moss, they would be entombed in earth forever. Their faces frozen in fear, mouths open and a scream forever stuck upon their lips.

She charged toward the park, intent on finding her wayward faerie. Once she got her hands on him, she would wrap them around his throat and shake him. How did he think this was the answer? Infect the world?

A police officer stepped in front of her with his hand outstretched. "Ma'am, I'm going to ask you to step aside. We're currently assessing the situation, and no civilians are allowed within the park. Please return to your home."

She didn't have time for this. Morgan snapped forward and touched a finger to his forehead. "You never saw me."

He flinched, but then a glassy eyed expression took the place of anger. "I never saw you."

"Thank you officer," she murmured as she slipped past him. "I hope I can save us all. And don't let anyone touch that moss!"

The moss touched her foot and traveled up her leg. It clung to her like a child, trying to push her away from the park but not devouring her as she'd seen it do in her vision.

"Leave me alone," she said. "I need to find him."

The moss pushed back harder.

Her time was limited. She had to find the damned Mountain King and hit him upside the head. Then she needed to kiss him, tell him she thought she was in love with him, and...

Well, she didn't have a plan beyond that. He just needed to know she was in love with him. And that she would stop at nothing to make sure he didn't hurt himself or anyone else. If that meant killing him, then she'd go with him.

But first, she had to deal with this ridiculous moss and grass shoving at her like a person.

"Enough," she growled. With a flex of her borrowed power, she pushed back at the growing things. They flinched at the touch of their master's magic.

One blade of grass still hung onto her foot. Frowning, she zapped it with more green magic.

"I'm here to help," she told the plants. "I don't want him to hurt any more than you do."

At least, she hoped that was the case.

"Please don't be sitting on that throne when I get there," she whispered as she slogged through thick grass and tangled moss. "Please, wait for me, Liam."

The trees had grown thicker. She'd once been to the city, though it was far from her home. This park had been her favorite place to visit because the trees were older than most parks. They told her stories of women who sat with their lovers having stuffy picnics where every word was a veiled promise.

They had always been kind to her. But now, they loomed as if they were trying to scare her. Trying to force her to leave before she found the man she loved.

Their trunks were ten times thicker. Squeezing between them became a feat of courage. She pressed her hand against a trunk and slid between the opening that grew smaller even as she blinked. "I just want to see him," she begged. "Please let me see him."

Their whispers weren't kind anymore. They were hostile and cruel. They said she didn't deserve to be here, not with the Mountain King. Witches weren't allowed to hold space with faeries.

She slapped a branch that reached down and yanked her hair. "Let me through!"

A blast of green magic scared the rest of the plants off. They let her run through the forest until her lungs screamed for breath and her legs ached.

She reached the top of the hill where she knew he was. She didn't know how, but she could feel him there.

He knelt before a throne made of the ancient tree at the center of the park. He was well and truly the Green Man. The mantle, the crown, every bit of him covered in flowers and moss.

His glowing green eyes looked up at the throne. He straightened and started toward the cursed seat.

Without thinking, Morgan threw herself from the brush and out into the open. Her scream echoed through the forest and silenced every hush of leaf and crack of branch. "Stop! Liam, stop!"

25

———————

He didn't even look back at her. Why wouldn't Liam look at her?

Morgan reached for him, fingers spread wide, arm stretching until her shoulder ached. She tried to run down the hill, but couldn't. Grass tangled around her legs, reaching up to her knees, grasping at her thighs. Vines spread from the trees and looped around her arms. The forest held her in place, forcing her to watch as the man she loved approached the throne.

There wasn't time for her to worry. There wasn't time for her to think.

All she could do was try one more time. Morgan felt her own magic bubbling up inside her. She was the forest. She was the plants. Everything in them was under her power, and she could take what she needed to get his attention.

A blast of witch magic pulsed from her body in a grand circle that burned the surrounding grass. The vines shrank away from her. Their pain filled screams made her ears bleed.

But it was her magic now. Not his magic, the kind she'd sucked from the elemental and that prevented her from moving. This magic running through her arms and into her fingertips was all Morgan's.

She'd made the sacrifice. Now, it was her turn to cast a spell upon the forest.

Dropping into a crouch, she pressed her hands into the ground. "Earth quake and dirt part, stop the man who owns my heart."

Black singed the grass in long veins, reaching out for Liam. The ground shook, quaking with the power of her magic and burning like a wildfire. The darkness reached him just as he lifted his foot for the last step to the throne.

Her magic caught him around the ankle, tugging his entire leg back to the earth and forcing him to take a knee before the throne once again. Breathing hard, she trembled as power drained from her.

The darkness held, but shook with the force of holding him in place. Her magic was no match for an elemental. She couldn't stop the Green Man from taking the throne, but she could give herself time to reach his side.

Reaching into the ground with her magic again, Morgan pulled from the life around her. The screaming of plants would haunt her dreams for decades. She would not stop, though. They were as much a part of her as breathing, but he was more important now.

She flew across the park toward the tree. Toward him. Toward the man who should have trusted her, and should have known she wouldn't drag him away from his purpose.

His glowing green gaze found hers. He stared at her as though she were a demon come to claim his soul. As though she would stop him from fulfilling a destiny that had been written into the very fabric of time.

And in a way, she supposed she was.

Morgan paused five feet from him. The twilight of her

magic spread, soaking in the debt of the dead plants she'd killed to save their king.

Tears filled her eyes. "Liam," she whispered.

"You may call me the Mountain King," he growled.

"No, I don't want to talk to you. I want to talk with Liam."

He shook his head. The crown of branches rattled. "We are one and the same now, witch."

It was worse than she'd thought. He'd given in to the elemental and now, what could she do?

Her legs shook, weak with emotion until they gave out. She fell onto her knees before him but still reached out her hands for Liam to take. He had to be in there somewhere.

He didn't take her hands.

"You don't have to do this," she whispered. "I know the magic is overwhelming and that you lose control. But you don't have to do this alone."

"I am never alone. The forest breathes life into me and I it."

The trees swayed above them. Their branches cracked with agreement. The Mountain King, the Earthen King, the Lord of the Spring Court would never be alone as long as their roots stretched into the ground.

Through the din of the forest chanting, she leaned closer and whispered, "I know how lonely it is to be lost in the forest, desperate for someone to just hold your hand. Liam, if you're still in there, I need you to listen to me."

He tugged his leg out of the darkness. Her magic strained, pulling at her very soul to contain him.

Morgan gasped in pain. Her sharp inhalation made him pause, although she didn't know if it was in fear of hurting her or merely because he was surprised.

The Mountain King stared down at her with a question in his eyes. "You're using your own magic to stop me."

"I couldn't defeat you with your magic," she replied.

"Once my magic is in you, it's yours. You can do whatever

you want with it. That's the price I pay for you to flourish." His brows furrowed, wrinkling between his eyes. "Why won't you just use it?"

"It's not a fair price." Morgan placed her palms against the ground and channeled more energy until her entire body shook like a leaf.

The elemental watched her with shock and discomfort. "Stop doing that."

She couldn't. She wouldn't. Liam would not move any closer to that throne, no matter how much of herself she had to give. Morgan shook her head to clear her mind. Her thoughts were suddenly foggy, unfocused as she gave more and more of herself.

"You will kill yourself witch. You can't keep casting the spell."

If she died to save the city, the entire human realm, then she would do so. For the first time in her life, Morgan wanted to do something worthwhile. She flexed her fingers in the dirt. Her soul stretched thin, like an elastic band held far too taut. It might snap if she kept going. But maybe that was okay.

Hands reached for hers, holding them between warm fingers. She looked up, hoping beyond hope that Liam would stare back at her.

But it was still those glowing green eyes. The eyes filled with power and so much confusion it made her chest ache.

"You can't stop me," he murmured. His grip tightened around her hands, not painful but comforting. "You cannot stop what will happen. The world will be a better place. Liam ensured the witches would remain alive, as the last remnants of humanity."

"We aren't human." Her vision turned foggy, but she had a feeling her power wasn't holding the elemental anymore. How had he gotten so close to her? He was supposed to be five feet away. "And this world needs humans in it."

"The world would be a better place without them."

"No, it wouldn't. I've tried to explain it to you, but you won't listen."

The elemental's green magic pressed against her mind. She didn't think he was trying to see into her soul or understand her reasoning. Instead, she was certain he would try to control her. To force her to stop when all she needed to do was continue forward.

Morgan slammed down the doors of her mind, locking them tight and throwing more magic into that then she did the ground.

"You cannot win," the elemental said. He stood up with the creaking sound of wind in tree branches. "Though your fight is remarkable."

He was leaving. He was walking toward the throne again, and she would lose him for real this time. But she was so tired. So...

Morgan fell onto her side in the blackened dirt. Her shoulder crunched against a stone, the pain blinding for a moment but awakening her just in time to see his foot touch the bottom step of the throne.

She remembered all the best things about the humans. How they helped each other even when they didn't think the other person deserved help. How people would buy an extra coffee to bring to the homeless man outside. She'd even seen them pick up trash from the beach, protest against beached whales, and grow herb gardens in their kitchen because they didn't understand their need to be closer to something wild.

She'd hated them, but had it been jealousy? Had she just wanted what they had?

He took another step up to the throne.

Visions of Liam flashed through her memories. His smile when she first attacked him and he realized she'd be a challenge. The grin on his face as he watched the green faeries dance atop the table. The soft way he touched her hair when he said she deserved better than him. The tender touch of his fingers against her heart every time they made love.

And in remembering all these things, she also remembered what it was like to be human.

She couldn't let him do this. Liam would sacrifice all he was for a goal he didn't want.

With a guttural scream, she slammed her hand against the ground. She didn't take from the earth this time. She gave it all her anguish and rage. All her disappointment in its king and the bright glimmering light of love burning in her chest every time she saw him.

Morgan gave it the gift of human emotions she hadn't felt in centuries. Feelings she had forced herself to forget so she could become one of the magic creatures. Feelings she'd been born with and had forgotten long ago.

And the earth swallowed it up.

It lapped at her emotions like she'd poured sweet wine upon it. The ground shivered with the weight of love. It quaked with the bitter taste of fear. And it split in two at the horrific sadness of losing him.

The earth opened up in a great crack that echoed through the forest like thunder. It broke between her and Liam. The ground shattered like glass under his foot and one dark tendril of witch magic reached up and wrapped around his foot.

The Mountain King paused, shook his leg, then realized he couldn't free it from the grasp of her magic.

He heaved a great, annoyed sigh. "Why are you doing this, witch? Just give up."

Laying on the ground, all she could do was stare at him. Her body shook with exhaustion and sadness. Morgan felt all her energy drain.

That was it.

That was all she had left.

Blowing out a breath, she licked her lips and replied, "Because I love you. I don't know how to explain it, but I do. More than life itself."

Another crack of thunder made her ears ache. She couldn't cover them with her hands, so instead she suffered through the ringing in her head.

When she could hear again, she noted the crunch of dead grass. The Mountain King knelt beside her and gently lifted her into his lap.

When she blinked, she stared up into the warm green eyes she'd fallen so desperately in love with. The elemental had retreated. Her Liam, her Mountain King, had returned.

"Oh thank god," she muttered, slumping. "I didn't think I would get you back."

"I didn't think you were so foolish you'd try to take your own life," he grumbled. His hands smoothed along her sides, easing over her sore muscles and shaking limbs. "What were you thinking, fool woman?"

"You planned to take the throne."

"But I wasn't leaving you."

Morgan reached up and cupped his cheek, holding him in place so he had to look at her. "You were leaving me. Don't pretend you weren't. You were about to take the coward's way out so you didn't have to feel pain anymore."

He winced. "It breaks my heart to hear you say that."

"And it breaks mine to know you would sacrifice an entire world because you don't have faith in them." Morgan slid her hand to the back of his neck and tugged him lower. "Trust me, Liam. Let the humans have this realm and let them fix it. Slowly, yes, but they will."

"I don't know how." A single tear formed in his eyes. The drop fell onto her cheek and slid down into her hair.

Morgan leaned up and pressed her lips against his. "I will teach you. Did you not hear me, you idiot? I love you. I love you so much I can barely breathe sometimes, and I can't go on without you."

"I heard you." He kissed her back, his lips warm and soft. "But I fear I don't deserve that love."

"Love isn't about deserving. It's about giving a piece of yourself and trusting the other person won't break it." She stroked the high peak of his cheekbone. "And I know you won't break me, Liam."

"Oh, my love," he whispered. "What am I going to do with you?"

Morgan opened her mouth to reply, only to pause. Green magic flooded through her body. It healed all her hurts, pushing through sore muscles and aching bones. It filled the well of her magic, which had been bone dry. She could feel it on the tips of her fingers. Spreading and soothing everything it touched.

He stopped too soon.

Shaking her head in denial, Morgan said, "No. You cannot contain all the magic of the elemental. Give me more, Liam."

"It will kill you."

"It won't." She could feel it bubbling inside her but not burning. "I can hold it. You don't have to be alone, Liam."

Liam leaned away from her, a question in his gaze. "Was this your plan all alone?"

Morgan didn't think it had been. She wasn't even sure they could do this now, let alone a few moments ago. But if he was overwhelmed by the amount of power in him, then let her use it. Together, they could temper the elemental and create new life.

"No," she admitted. "But it's my plan now."

He didn't hesitate. Liam released all the magic he could into her body. She tossed her head back, and the world turned green.

Magic, so pure and so raw, flowed through her veins like

roots. It tangled around her heart and soul, becoming one piece that solidified into an emerald in her chest. This was the magic she'd always desired. Magic she knew she could control if only she took the throne.

But she didn't want a throne. All Morgan wanted was a quiet life, in a little cottage, with faeries at her feet.

Morgan sent all the overflowing power into the ground. She healed the burned grass. She fed the trees and the flowers until a meadow burst to life around them, flowering and enticing bees to dance on every petal.

And when she was done, all the power that had burned through Liam quieted. The green glow in his eyes dimmed. Even the crackle of magic at his fingertips was gone.

He leaned over her, breathing hard with his mouth agape. "It's gone," he whispered.

"For good?"

"No, just... asleep." His eyes widened in shock. "You tamed it."

"We tamed it." Morgan squeezed his bicep, reassuring him with her body as her vision blurred. The magic had taken its toll on her body, not painfully so, but it had made her exhausted. "Take me home, Liam. To the little cottage you built with mud faeries and sassy snakes."

"I thought you said you wanted to stay here?" He scooped her up into his arms, lifting her as he stood. "You wanted normality and humankind."

"I was wrong," she whispered. "I just want you."

26

L iam stretched his arms over his head, listening to the crack of his spine in the crisp morning air. Birds sang in the distance along with the wind rustling through the trees. He'd just finished chopping the last bit of wood for winter.

Each piece was done by hand. He ensured the trees knew that even though they were dead, their pieces would assist their king.

Of course, he also had a queen now who constantly planted seedings in every open spot. His lips curled in pleasure. She liked it here far more than he'd thought she would.

Morgan had been so forthright in wanting to live in the human realm for the rest of her life, he'd thought she'd put up a fight coming here. No one wanted to feel as though they were in a prison, so he kept the portals open for her.

Always.

He rounded the house with a grin on his face. He'd been doing that lately. Smiling like he hadn't a care in the world.

In a way, he supposed he didn't anymore. The elemental remained quiet and pleased in his head. Though the creature still swelled with power, there was now an outlet. A way for Liam to control the beast and satisfy the creature who had wanted nothing more than destruction.

The door to their cabin opened, and Morgan stepped out to greet him. Arcane curled around her bicep, his head on her shoulder and eyes closed as he enjoyed the heat of the sun.

But it was the smile on her face that made his soul soar. They hadn't really gotten to know each other before all this. Not when she was trying to kill him and he was trying to end the world.

Now, they had the space to learn and grow. They could ask the silly questions like what was her favorite color and did she want flowers or jewels?

He'd asked more questions every single day, wanting to absorb every aspect of who she was.

His pace quickened until he was right in front of her. Liam scooped her up by the waist and tugged her against his chest. Growling under his breath, he leaned down and inhaled the rose petal scent of her hair. "What is your favorite sweet treat, queen of mine?"

"Oh, today's question is about candy?" she asked. She tossed her head back and shook the long mane of her ebony hair. "Truffles," she replied. "Chocolate truffles."

"With caramel centers?"

"No, vanilla. Rather boring like that I suppose."

He couldn't imagine a single aspect of her was boring, no matter how much she wanted to convince him. He lifted her up into the air, feet dangling and laughing dancing through the air. "Vanilla sounds lovely. Especially drizzled atop these beautiful, wonderful pillows."

He pressed a kiss against her revealed chest, only to hear her squeal. She always shouted like that. As if the sound wasn't temptation enough for him to lick his tongue through the crevice.

"Liam!" she shouted. "Stop it!"

In his ear, he heard an answering hiss. "Yes, please. Stop that."

Ah, right. Arcane.

Hysterical laughter echoed from within the cottage, and one of Monstera's roots poked out of the ground. Clearly his old friend was enjoying herself.

Cheeks burning, Liam placed Morgan back onto the ground and patted Arcane's head. "Sorry old friend."

"I'm not invisible," the snake muttered. "I'm right here. I've always been here and instead, you're just ignoring me."

"I'm not ignoring you."

"Ignoring." Arcane released his hold on Morgan's arm and slithered down to the ground. Flicking his tongue at them, he moved off through the garden while grumbling about inappropriate lovebirds.

Morgan chuckled.

She looked so lovely in this place he'd created. Her hair glimmered in the sunlight, black giving way to shades of blue and violet. She'd taken to wearing clothing similar to his own. Billowy peasant shirts in shades of white and cream tucked into tight, dark pants that made his mind run wild with ideas. Most involving peeling them off her long legs and licking his way back up.

Distracting. That was the only word for a woman like her.

Her arms were full of vine clippings today. English ivy tangled through her hair and made a crown atop her head like a wreath. She grinned up at him and tilted her head to the side. "Done already?"

"With what?" He hadn't the faintest idea what she was talking about.

"Chopping wood."

"Ah." Right, he'd been doing that only a few moments ago.

She always made his mind wander. Liam scratched the back of his neck and nodded. "Done."

"Good, you can help me plant these then." She deposited an entire armful of plants into his waiting grip and wiped her hands on her hips.

He shifted all the ivy and reached out to touch a finger to her cheek. Green magic flowed from him into her. This was how they always managed it now. Just a tiny bit, whenever he saw her. Enough to take the edge off and enough to share.

Morgan smiled and pressed a kiss against his fingertip. "We have work to do, love."

"Love," he said, his voice a guttural groan. "You know how much I adore it when you call me that."

Her grin was wicked and full of pleasurable promises. "Oh I know. I love it just as much as you do." She nodded toward the garden. "Now go plant those in the ground around the house. They've been in glass jars all week and are more than ready for their new home. Plants first."

All the faeries in the world didn't hold a candle to his green witch who knew how to spread love wherever she went.

Liam tromped over to the side of the house, but not before he saw her spin around and lift a mud faerie into the air. It had a strange glint of metal tucked against the lily pad atop its head.

"You again!" she shouted, her voice too loud to be angry. "What did I tell you about sneaking through the garden?"

As she tossed the mud faerie up into the air and caught it gently in her arms, he realized this was what he'd been missing.

Liam might have created a realm for the Mountain King, but he'd never had a family.

Not until now.

Not until her.

EPILOGUE

Read on for a sneak peek of the next book, King of the Frost

The children screamed on the swing set, kicking their feet up to the clouds and shouting to the high heavens. For a second, Ayla didn't see their cheerful faces. She saw war ragged expressions, haunted and horrified children who knew their parents weren't coming home.

Not now, not ever.

Shaking her head, she waved a hand. "Don't swing too high! Remember what I said!"

Her nephew only kicked his feet with more purpose. "Auntie Ayla! I'm a big boy now. I can go higher than all the other kids!"

Maybe he could, but that didn't mean he wouldn't rip out her heart with every movement. Maybe this was why her brother wanted Ayla to watch the twins rather than any other nanny. She couldn't bear the thought of them hurting themselves. It was like taking out a piece of her own heart.

Of course, she'd always been like this. Even in the waiting room of the hospital, she'd paced back and forth. Her heart had hammered between her ribs and she'd sent prayers to a God she didn't believe.

"Please let them live," she had said repeatedly. "If you ever thought kindly of my people, or if I've ever done anything in your light, let them live."

Ian and Ivan were born on the winter solstice like princes to Ayla's fairytale. Although, when they were out and about, she called them gremlins. They loved to cause trouble wherever they went. She could always read the mischief in their expressions.

Ayla sometimes saw other faces laid over theirs. Little monsters who crawled out of the shadows and unlaced shoes, poured sugar out of bowls, and kicked dust bunnies out from under the couch.

When she was very little, she hadn't understood the strange

thoughts that sometimes appeared in her mind. Her brother, Henry, had been far more understanding. When her parents had called her visions an overactive imagination, he'd called it genius.

Ayla had always been his little "faerie" sister. Because he'd seen the faeries come and put her in her bed, swapping out his real sister for her.

Their parents hadn't been fond of the nickname. In fact, they'd done everything they could to discourage him from calling her that. Even though Ayla quite liked being called a faerie.

It wasn't until she was much older before she realized how right he'd been.

Even now she could see the faeries from where she sat. Two phookas played with the boys. Ian and Ivan had no idea there was magic around them, but they noticed the wind tickling their hair. They couldn't see the cat-like faeries teasing them. Still, the boys played with them, nonetheless.

Maybe that's why she loved the twins so much. They had a bit of magic in them, even though they were one hundred percent human.

She sighed and set her purse on the bench next to her. They were lucky to have the entire park to themselves today, a rare moment when there were usually teems of children shrieking for their parents to push them higher. At least it meant she could leave her things where they were.

Ayla wandered toward the boys, intent on giving them a shove to send them flying up into the air. Except, she noticed a broad figure in white off in the distance. He stood by the hedges and stared at them, his gaze intense and shadowed.

Every hair on her body stood up on end. Was this man trying to case out her nephews? Was he trying to... what? Kidnap them?

Over her dead body. These boys were protected by a nanny with a lot more tricks up her sleeve than any normal human.

She meandered to the swing set with her eyes on the male figure. "Here," she said, her voice jubilant but her jaw clenched. "Let me give you a push."

Ivan shrieked in happiness, his voice like a balm to her soul. Did he know how much she loved him? Probably. But she didn't think the boys would ever realize just how far she'd go to protect them. Not a single hair on their head could be lost without her mourning.

"Boys?" she asked. They both turned their heads toward her, trying to pretend they were listening while still kicking their feet. "I'm going to go over there and talk with that man. Okay? Stay where you are, please. Don't make me come find you like last time."

Ian and Ivan liked to play tricks. The gremlins thought hiding on her was the greatest fun they could ever have, even though it made her want to cry.

"Okay, auntie!" Ivan said, ignoring her.

"What man?" Ian asked. He slowed his swinging just enough to crane his neck and look where she pointed. "I don't see anyone?"

The air in her lungs froze. Her heart raced in her ears, thumping hard like the beat of a drum. Ayla could feel the blood drain from her face.

Don't let the boys see you upset, she thought to herself.

Children didn't understand fear. Nor should they.

Ayla squared her shoulders and plastered a fake grin on her face. "Well, maybe you don't see him. But I do!"

Ian giggled and rocked on the swing to get it moving again. He'd never know there actually was a man standing there, staring at the boys as though he wanted to devour them.

She shivered. Faeries used to eat human children in the old days.

If this faerie thought he'd get his teeth on her boys, then he had another thing coming. She clenched her hands into fists and stalked to the corner of the park.

The closer she got, the more details she could see about this strange man. He wasn't wearing a white suit as she had originally thought. His entire body was wrapped in bandages. A few of the tails had wiggled loose, or perhaps he'd jostled them free. They danced in the wind as she approached, whispering of pain and battle.

The bandages even covered his face other than one cream colored eye. He followed her movement, waiting for her to reach him without attempting to rush her.

"What do you want?" she snapped when she finally stood in front of him. She crossed her arms over her chest and blew a strand of pale hair from her face.

"My queen," the faerie said. He dropped into a low bow, but it was his voice that made her skin crawl. The deep sound was the bellows of wind rushing through a canyon. He was one of her own kind. An air faerie who had somehow made his way to the human realm.

"I'm no one's queen," Ayla replied. "I'm a nanny, as you can clearly see. The boys are mine."

"You've had children?" He snapped up straight as an arrow. "We were unaware there were princes."

She shook her head. "No, they are my brother's. But they are important to me."

"Brother?" The strange faerie pressed a hand against his chest. "You have no siblings, Ayla of Frostborn."

Sure. They might think she was the queen of their people, but clearly she wasn't. Her family had cast her aside, sent her to live with humans because she was worth nothing to them. They'd rather trade her for a human child. A slave.

Ayla had been forced to grow up thinking she was human. She could do things the other kids couldn't. Make the wind rustle her hair, turn the air frosty, make snow fall from the sky on a whim. She wasn't like the humans and she'd scared them because of it.

She'd only realized what she was because an errant faerie had told her when she'd turned sixteen. Horns grew atop his head and his feet were hooves.

"You're a changeling child," he'd said with a leer. "No one wanted you, so they sent you away to live with the humans. Poor dear. You'll never even know who your parents are."

Until much later, when her parents had died, and the court shifted power to someone new. Then they all wanted her back.

She had her pride.

Shifting her stance, she cocked her hip out to the side. "I'm not interested. I've told a hundred people before you. He can keep the throne. I don't want it."

The faerie dropped to his knees, shuffling forward with bandages snapping in a sudden wind. "Please, my queen. Your people are dying, and we need you to save us."

"I'm no savior, and I'm no queen." Ayla turned to leave. He could stay on his knees as long as he wanted, but she wouldn't go with him. The boys needed her. The family needed her. And that was more than any faerie had given her.

He flinched and shuffled forward again, reaching out and grasping onto the hem of her button down yellow shirt. "Please, mistress. At least hear me. The mad king took the throne when your parents died, but none of us knew what would happen if he did. The air court is dying. He is killing us all."

"Then find someone to stop him. Surely there are a hundred faeries out there willing to do the job." She shook him off her shirt. "Let go."

"No, my queen. No one can stop him; we've tried. He is all powerful and holds within him an elemental who wants to destroy the human realm. If you don't stop him, if you don't take back what is rightfully yours, then it won't just be the faeries who die. It will be everyone. The whole world."

She could only imagine this was the newest tactic to get her to come home. Faeries attacking humans? They wouldn't. They didn't have the resources.

Ayla snorted and tried to peel his hands off her shirt. "Nice try. Maybe tell the next guy threatening my family was a bad idea."

"I'm not threatening anyone!" he shouted. "I'm telling you the truth. If the elemental takes over the king, then we are all lost. All the faerie kings, all those who rule the Season courts, will soon be overwhelmed. This is how the world ends, my queen. And you are the only one who can stop it."

His words settled on her shoulders like an omen. She hated to admit he'd gotten into her head, but the man definitely had. Somehow, he'd made her nervous.

Glancing over her shoulder, she made sure the boys were still on the swings. When she had ensured they were behaving, she turned back to the man and held onto his hands with a firm grip. "I don't know if you're telling the truth or not, but I'm not the person you're looking for."

Ayla released his hands and left him on the ground. The faerie hung in his head in defeat, but she tried not to let it bother her too much. The faeries had their own problems. They weren't hers just because she shared blood with two people who hadn't wanted her.

Still, her stomach rolled with guilt. Her breakfast of syrupy pancakes pressed against the back of her throat, but she refused to vomit in the trashcan. She had a family to protect. Two nephews who loved her. A brother and a sister-in-law who were kind enough to pay her and let her live in the little cottage behind their house. Ayla was blessed with so much, she didn't need to worry about faeries.

"Come on, boys!" she shouted. "We're going home!"

Though the twins complained, they hopped off the swing set and raced toward her bag. Ian grabbed her purse and held it open for Ivan to rummage through, looking for her car keys.

They held up the keys with two sticky grins long before she reached their side. Kneeling, Ayla gathered them close to her chest and squeezed them tight.

"I love you two," she whispered. "You know that, right?"

They wiggled and in unison replied, "We know Auntie Ayla! Let go!"

It was always the same with the two of them. They hated getting snuggled or loved now that they were older.

She plucked the keys from Ivan's hands and pointed to the car. "Car boys. Let's go home."

ABOUT THE AUTHOR

Elizabeth Frost is the pen name of USAToday Bestselling author Emma Hamm. You'll find these stories to be steamy paranormal/urban fantasy, whereas the ones under Emma Hamm will be less steamy and more traditional fantasy worlds.

So if you want spice, you want Frost ;)

 facebook.com/EmmaHammAuthor

 twitter.com/EmmaHammAuthor

 instagram.com/emmahammauthor